CALYPSO

STORIES OF THE CARIBBEAN

BY RICHARD DAYBELL

CARIBE BOOKS

LOVE and loss, sex and skullduggery, conquests, failures, foibles – these are the elements of calypso, the stories in song that personify the islands of the West Indies. Calypso's origins and rhythms are African, but somewhere along the way they were seduced by the innocence of the Caribbean. Originally a medium of communication among the poor, calypso stories were originally sung by the chantwell, a sort of town crier who provided information spiced with social commentary. Over the years, the commentary became the driving force, and the story-songs sought to entertain, amuse, and poke fun at everything from errant spouses to jaded northern tourists attempting to step out of their button-down world into the leisurely pace of the islands. The following stories also seek to entertain, amuse, and poke fun, particularly at those of us who think we have a corner on reality.

STONE COLD DEAD
IN DE MARKET

Upton Swann sat all alone on the ornate cast iron love seat that had been painted white sometime in the distant past, shaded by a spreading Poinciana, surrounded by chattering merchants with piles of bananas to the right, piles of coconuts to the left – fruits, vegetables, fish and tourists everywhere. Activity swirled around him, but he didn't seem to care. It was noon. He'd been sitting there since 7 a.m.

On a second floor terrace of the Hotel Vieux Habitant that overlooked the market square, five people sat in a row, leaning over the railing, staring down past the frenzied activity at Upton Swann. They, too, had been sitting there since seven.

Upton Swann and his audience of five had all been together on the terrace the previous evening, enjoying the serenity of the market square, abandoned in the early evening hours by merchants and tourists alike. And they enjoyed the soft warmth tempered by the steady breeze off the ocean – at least five of them did; Upton Swann did not. He found the climate foul – too hot – and that was just the tip of his iceberg of complaints about this island in particular and the Caribbean in general. Unlike the others he could not wait to get back to the sensible climate of New York in March, a desire he did not endeavor to keep to himself. "What if I get sick here?" he lamented. "My god, they've probably got chickens wandering through the hospital."

By 8 p.m., he had enjoyed just about as much of the tropical night as he intended to enjoy. With a harrumph, he marched inside, revved the air conditioner up to its maximum, and sat down on the couch with a tumbler of Scotch. Within minutes, he would complain no more.

The beginning of Upton Swann's journey to the great beyond went unnoticed. In fact, he was about two hours along before the Dexters – Howard and Wilma – came in and thought it odd that the tumbler lay in his lap in the center of a large Scotch stain. (Later, they would recall that his last words were: "This is a wretched place; I need Scotch." Not eloquent enough for his tombstone, but certainly better than Myrna Pomeroy's first husband's last words: "Five minutes on the toilet and I'll be just fine.")

The Dexters sounded a general alarm, and Myrna, her current husband Phil Pomeroy, and Upton's widow Adele all came running in – although Adele didn't yet realize that she was a widow, not until Howard Dexter said: "He's deader than a doornail."

Adele sobbed, and the others looked on with bewildered expressions. Howard wasn't a coroner or a doctor or anything, but he knew a lot of things, and the others accepted his diagnosis.

"Do you suppose he had a heart attack?" asked

Myrna Pomeroy.

Howard Dexter picked up the bottle of scotch and ceremoniously sniffed at it. He might have been selecting a wine for their dinner. Then he poured a few drops into his palm, wetted a finger and touched it to his tongue. The others watched in silence.

"Poison," Howard proclaimed. "Not a doubt of it. This Scotch has really been laced with it." Howard wasn't a pharmacologist or detective either, but he knew a lot of things.

Adele sobbed again, and Myrna Pomeroy said: "How could it be? We were all here. How could someone have... no, you're not suggesting...?"

"One of us killed him," said Howard. "No other answer. We had the opportunity, and nobody else on this island even knew him."

"But why?" asked Wilma Dexter, looking at her husband who knew a lot of things.

"Why not might be more the answer," said Howard. "Did any of us really like him? Even Adele?" No one answered. "I, myself, as his partner, gain full control of the business. Adele stands to inherit a tidy sum, I imagine. And she's earned it, the way he's treated her."

"He has my promissory note for $200,000," offered Phil Pomeroy, looking surprised, even as he spoke, that he was throwing himself in. "A so-called loan between friends, but at a very unfriendly rate of interest. The man was a shark."

The conversation quickly became a group confessional. Wilma Dexter, giving her husband, then Adele, quick sheepish looks, said quietly: "He put the moves on me more than once. He was fairly disgusting."

"Oh dear," said Adele.

"Me too," said Myrna. "Just this afternoon."

They all looked at the corpse, as though seeing the totality of his corruption and vileness for the first time – although he didn't look all that corrupt and vile at the moment with his face twisted into a silly little grin and a tumbler of Scotch in his lap. Then they began to look suspiciously at each other, sizing each other for murderer's shoes. "Would anyone care to confess?" said Howard. No one volunteered. "I guess we'll have to call the police."

"Do we have to?" asked Adele. "They're... they're foreigners. They'd be happy to just throw one of us in a stinky jail and be done with it."

"Or all of us," added Wilma Dexter.

"Does it really matter who did it?" asked Phil Pomeroy. "I mean, when you really get right down to it, there's no great loss." Adele sobbed again, and they all weighed Phil's words.

"I guess Phil's right," said Adele. She shivered. "He was brutish, and I'm well rid of him. It's just... just so ghoulish to be talking about him this way. And he's sitting right here." She looked at her dead husband and suddenly giggled. "Wouldn't we all be terribly embarrassed if he were just pretending to be dead?" They all studied the body once more just to be certain, and it gradually dawned on each of them that just not telling the police didn't solve their problem. Their problem was sitting on the couch.

The eventual plan was, of course, Howard's, and it centered on the theory that if the body were found in a crowded public place, like say the market, with hundreds of people around – but not a certain fivesome – the police, who were probably incompetent anyway, would assume he died of natural causes, especially when they brought the bad news to his wife and friends and learned of his history of a bad heart.

Howard's idea came under fire, however, as the morning wore on and nobody paid any attention to the dead man on the love seat in the market. What few words were spoken on the terrace during that tense morning were given toward characterization of, first, Howard's idea, then his know-it-all attitude, and, lastly, his parentage.

At one-thirty, a native woman and her young daughter joined Upton Swann on the love seat. The woman looked straight ahead, minding her own business just as though he weren't there, but the little girl looked inquisitively up at Upton's face. "Mama, he's so white," she said.

"Hush," said her mama, quickly standing and pulling her wide-eyed daughter away with her. Wilma Dexter squirmed in her chair.

At three, a young boy asked Upton Swann for a *dollah* and, when Swann didn't answer, made an obscene gesture and scurried off. Phil Pomeroy sighed, stood, went inside, and mixed a pitcher of martinis.

At 4:15, a shaggy, rather ragged, man carrying a bottle-shaped paper bag weaved unsteadily through the crowd and plopped down on the love seat. By 4:30, he was engaged in a lively conversation with Upton, laughing, gesturing broadly, and occasionally slapping him on the knee. The somewhat one-sided conversation lasted until 5 o'clock when the man stood, said "See you around, buddy," and wandered off.

Adele groaned, Phil went for more martinis, and Wilma growled at her husband: "This is all your fault, you know."

"Me?" said Howard with a look of disbelief. "I didn't kill him."

"I'm not so sure," said Wilma. "It would be just like you."

"Stop, stop," said Adele. "I'll go tell them I did it. You all think I did it, anyway. I'll confess and go to the stinky jail. At least it will all be over."

"No you won't," said Myrna. "We don't all think you did it. We'll just wait. It was a stupid plan, but we'll just have to wait. Everything will be all right."

"It will," seconded Howard. "And now it really doesn't matter who actually killed him. We're all equally guilty."

"I'll drink to that," said Phil. He raised his glass toward the market. "To the corpse." They all downed martinis.

At 6, they thought maybe their vigil would finally end. Upton was leaning to the left, barely noticeable at first, but before long with a decided tilt. They watched, five chins on the railing, as gravity took hold, and Upton rolled to his side, lying across the love seat. And he had not been horizontal for three minutes when a policeman appeared. The gang of five looked at one another excitedly, then sat back in their chairs so as not to draw the policeman's attention to the terrace.

The policeman approached the slumped over Upton Swann and said in a firm voice: "Hey mon, no sleeping here. You take yourself home now." He gave Upton a couple of taps with his nightstick. "Get along now. If you're not gone when I get back, you'll do your sobering up in a jail cell." He sauntered away, and spirits flagged on the terrace.

The policeman didn't return, and darkness enveloped the market square with Upton Swann still lying on the love seat. Adele Swann went to bed and sobbed herself to sleep. The others found sleep in various positions on the floor, except for Phil Pomeroy, who technically passed out while dressing down the sleeping Howard Dexter.

They were back on the terrace before dawn, straining eyes to determine whether Upton Swann still lay there in the darkness. As the sky lightened, the darkness slowly dissipated and, to their great disappointment, they were able to discern a familiar shape on the love seat. But with the steady brightening of the dawn, they became aware of a marked difference down there in the market – Upton Swann was still there all right, but he was stark naked.

The man who had gone unnoticed in the market for a full 24 hours would not go unnoticed another day. By 7, a crowd had formed around the naked body on the love seat, and by 7:30, the police had whisked Upton Swann away.

The relief on the terrace was short-lived, as apprehension quickly whisked it away. A naked American tourist has a heart attack in the market – it didn't have quite the air of authenticity they sought. Finally, late that afternoon, Adele was summoned to the police station. Her friends accompanied her to act as chorus.

"Do you have any idea why your husband would be naked and dead in the market?" the police chief asked tactfully.

Adele sobbed and grew flustered. The others were certain she was going to say something stupid that would send them all to jail. "Didn't you tell us, Adele," said Howard, stepping in to save the day, "that Upton had a sleepwalking prob – ?"

"I do have an idea," said the police chief, ignoring Howard. "Actually, it's more than an idea; it's an iron-tight conclusion. Our coroner made a careful examination, did tests."

The five culprits were sweating now, and it wasn't from the tropical warmth. "He had," Howard recited, "a history of heart . . ."

"Naturally, when we find a naked dead man, reeking of alcohol, we are suspicious. We sometimes even suspect foul play. That's why we were so thorough. But we found no evidence of foul play whatsoever."

"No foul play," Adele repeated mechanically.

"No foul play," said the police chief in a tone that suggested he would prefer no further interruptions. "As it turned out, he had a massive heart attack. Sat down on the bench and died. We caught the thief who stole his clothes. You can pick them up at the desk."

"A heart attack," said Howard, dumfounded. "Are you sure?"

"Absolutely."

As they filed out of the police station, Howard continued to mumble. "A heart attack. But I was so certain it was poison."

"No, Howard, just a heart attack," said Adele, with a little smile. "The police chief said so – a heart attack. Poor, poor Upton."

But nothing gets by the children who sing calypso in the market square:

Stone cold dead in de market, stone cold dead in de market,
Stone cold dead in de market, I killed nobody but me husband...

Island in the Sun

"Have sense, Santo," said Max-Anthony, the engineer. "You are only delaying the inevitable."

"It is inevitable that my tree should grow," answered Santo, refusing to budge from where he stood in front of his tree. "Grow to maturity and bear fruit."

Santo was quite proud of his tree. It was the only such tree on the entire island. People told him an olive tree would not grow here. Actually, they told him that it might grow very well, but that without chilly nights, it would never produce olives, just leaves. Santo didn't believe them. His tree had been growing for two years now, and it was a handsome tree. Such a handsome tree was bound to grow olives.

The tree was as tall as his three-year-old son. He wondered which of the two would grow faster, but now he would never know because Claudine had taken his son, had left him and returned to Provence. Now he had only the olive tree.

"You're a fool, Santo," said Max-Anthony, a man with little patience. "This hotel will be good for the island. It will create many jobs. Perhaps a job for you."

"I do not need a job," said Santo. "I have retired."

He had brought the olive tree here from Provence when it was just a tiny sapling. He had kept it hidden because it was probably an illegal thing to do. Did that make him a smuggler? Provence was a very pretty place, a place he had liked very much. And he had particularly loved the olive groves. It was under the canopy of an olive tree, that he and Claudine had spent their first time together. They delighted in the imperfection of its twisted trunk, the way the light played through it's shivering gray-green leaves, creating impressionistic patterns of light on the ground beside them. Their son had been conceived under that tree.

Pulled by the strings of young love – Claudine was young, Santo not so young – she had agreed that the three of them could return to the island, to the village of Santo's parents and grandparents, to that stretch of beach that had for a hundred years been theirs. But Claudine soon found that she could not tolerate island life; she needed more than it could give. She yearned for Provence, needed cities like Arles and Avignon, needed to be just a high-speed train ride from Paris. She begged him to return with her, but he couldn't. He belonged here, just as Claudine belonged in Provence.

The officials from the hotel company had come from their air-conditioned offices to plead with him as well, but Santo refused to go. "You are trespassing," said a Mr. Alexander through pursed lips in a pallid face. He wore a suit. "This beach belongs to the Caribe Development Corporation. We will have you removed. Forcibly, if necessary."

It had become important for Santo to be somewhere he belonged. So much of his life had been spent in places he didn't belong – first moving from one island to another, each one bigger and more indifferent – Statia, St. Vincent, then Trinidad – cutting cane and loading banana boats until finding work as a bartender. He was a good bartender; he knew how to charm the tourists, particularly the ladies, whom he flattered unabashedly. He moved on to Caracas, then Madrid and Barcelona, Algeria, and finally to southern France – to Provence, to the olive groves and to Claudine.

He had lost Claudine and his son, and now, in the name of progress, they wanted to take his tree. But this beach was his; they would not move him or his tree.

"This beach belongs to me; it has always belonged to my family."

"You're mistaken."

"I'm not mistaken," shouted Santo. "I have the papers." Santo waved the papers at Mr. Alexander.

"Those papers were issued by a government that no longer exists," said Max-Anthony, joining Mr. Alexander. "They are worthless, and you know it."

"Can you have him removed?" asked Mr. Alexander.

"Don't worry," said Max-Anthony. "He will move when the bulldozer comes. No more games, Santo."

Several days passed before the bulldozer arrived. During that time, Santo kept a constant vigil at the olive tree. During the day, tourists passing by would sometimes stop to talk to Santo. Most had already heard of the crazy man and his olive tree, but Santo's disarming smile and his friendliness would make them wonder whether he were crazy or merely a man with a cause, which is hardly so crazy. Knowing that he remained night and day at the tree, some would bring him food and would sit and talk with him while he ate.

The young couple from the south of England shivered as Santo told them about sleeping on the dock in Trinidad after loading a banana boat and awaking to find a fat tarantula sitting on his chest staring at him. The three ladies from California gushed over his tales of Spain during the last days of Generalissimo Franco. And the young Montrealer listened until well after midnight as Santo talked of his time in Algeria with the French Foreign Legion.

The bulldozer arrived early the next morning. Santo had to shake himself awake, and for a moment, he thought he was awaking from a nightmare in which he was about to be eaten by a huge yellow monster. But even with his eyes open, the yellow monster remained, growling at him.

"Go away, crazy one," shouted Luis Jordan from atop the chugging beast. Luis was a young man who had come to the island to do construction work; he didn't belong on the island. He was an angry, combative young man, frequently picking fights, and Santo didn't like him much. "You don't think I'll plow you down, do you, crazy man?"

"I am not crazy," answered Santo. "Go away."

"Don't be smart with me, crazy man. You won't stop me. I don't care if you live or die. You're trespassing. I can plow you under and nobody will say anything. I'll take down that damn tree, and I'll take you down with it. Believe me."

"I believe you."

"As you should," boasted Luis. "Now stand aside."

"I can't stand aside. This is my place. It was my mama's and my papa's, and it was their mama's and papa's. Go away and leave me alone."

"I warned you," said Luis, grinning as though he were really happy that Santo would not move, that he would have the pleasure of plowing him under. "Good riddance to your lunacy." The bulldozer's engine whined, and the beast lurched forward. Santo stood his ground as the yellow monster bore down on him, it's driver laughing. Santo closed his eyes.

The Crystal Coral Beach Club was a magnificent place. It straddled a mile's worth of white sand beach and bathed it in grandeur and opulence. Open for the first time this season, it was an unqualified success, drawing tourists from throughout the world and remaining fully occupied. Hopes were high that it would bring years of prosperity to the tiny island.

On this day, the first anniversary of groundbreaking for the beach club, a large throng of tourists had gathered together. The story of the Beach Club's shaky beginnings had traveled from the swimming pool to the tennis courts to the lounge and to the bright blue water and back. This was to be a celebration of that day of confrontation.

The olive tree had grown to nearly ten feet and was beautiful to behold; looking at this tree, it was hardly surprising that so many people considered olive trees holy. Santo emerged from the modest house just beyond the tree, a house flanked by hibiscus, bougainvillea, and the beach club's 156 luxury rooms. Santo the celebrity beamed as he joined the others at the tree and shared a toast with the couple from the south of England, the three ladies from California, the Montrealer, and the others who had been here last year, the ones who had ignored the metallic whine of impending doom to suddenly join Santo in front of his tiny tree, linking their arms with his in defiance of the bulldozer.

With a grin, Santo pointed to where, even though it defied all the rules of horticulture and all the laws of botany (but didn't surprise Santo or his friends one little bit), a single olive clung tenaciously to a branch of his olive tree.

WILL HIS LOVE BE
LIKE HIS RUM?

"Please, oh please," Caterina sobbed as she sat cross-legged in front of the closet, speaking to its door, a flat, lifeless wooden thing – albeit with a pretty brass knob – that, being but a door, would not or could not appreciate the beauty of the long legs folded in front of it. Long legs were common in her family, but Caterina's were the longest and most pleasantly proportioned. Nor could the door perceive the pout that played on the full red lips that also ran in the family but which once again reached perfection in Caterina.

And so too it was with raven tresses, flashing eyes and practically any other physical feature one might care to compare – Caterina had dipped deeply, and perhaps unfairly, into the gene pool. Even though the closet door could not appreciate the loveliness of the creature sitting before it, Etienne, who sat behind it, cross-legged as well, could, but would not – at least not during the past several hours of his self-imposed incarceration within the dark cubicle.

"Please Etienne," said Caterina, for in truth she spoke to him not to the door, as a passerby, were there one, might conclude. "Please come out." Caterina was certainly justified in her lament, since this should have been her night of nights, her wedding night, and not a night to be sitting in front of a closet, a closet whose only inhabitant was the man with whom she might more appropriately be sharing a conjugal bed, not a locked door.

"I can't," sniffed Etienne. This man in the closet was a young man who, everyone agreed, was the finest catch for a young woman in the entire valley, perhaps on the entire island. The closet notwithstanding, Caterina was one very fortunate young lady. Never mind that Etienne was handsome but not outrageously so, that he was smart and industrious but not fantastically clever, that he was interesting but not totally diverting. And never mind that Caterina was outrageously beautiful, as talented as she was beautiful, and as witty as she was talented. Never mind. It was she who was the lucky one.

Etienne now managed and would soon share with his twin brother, Hippolyte, ownership of the Buccaneer Rum Works, the island's leading manufacturer of spirits and its most successful business enterprise. Their father, who had inherited the company from his father, had thankfully retired after spending his last few working years dabbling with senility and seducing a string of shockingly young female employees.

As twins, Etienne and Hippolyte shared their appearance but little else. While Etienne took after their industrious father of his early years, Hippolyte aped his later years. And while he might be an equal catch to Etienne in theory, Hippolyte was expected by most observers to end up at the wrong end of an angry father's or jealous husband's shotgun long before he gave any thought to an exchange of wedding vows. Hippolyte had pursued

Caterina (as had most of the other young men in the valley), but since his pursuit was neither monogamous nor sustained, Caterina never gave it much thought. She had occasionally wondered what life with a rogue like Hippolyte would be – exciting probably, but tortuous. She was more comfortable with the stability of an Etienne.

She had not counted on the closet. After all, Caterina was a young woman with a very traditional set of desires, and while she had not come to this marriage as pure as the pristine sands of Coyaba Beach, she certainly had not engaged in enough sexual pleasure to now pledge herself at this early age to a life of celibacy by the closet door. For that was what had driven poor Etienne to the closet – a sudden fear of the marriage bed, a fear of the consummation and a fear of the very object of his desires.

The party that followed their picture-book wedding was loud and energetic, and as might be expected, the rum was plentiful. As the evening careened forward at an ever-greater velocity, the dancing and talking and laughing grew more animated, and the young men who insisted on kissing the bride over and over again grew friskier. They kissed more passionately, hugged more ambitiously and fondled more freely until the bride found herself becoming eager to explore that final item on the day's calendar of events. She took her new husband by the hand, announced to an enthusiastic cheer that they were going upstairs to do it now, and left the party.

When they were alone, Caterina began to pursue the timid Etienne shamelessly. But even though rum had clouded his mind, it had not put him enough at ease to prevent the overwhelming fear that her playfulness instilled. And when she disrobed, he bolted for the closet.

"You hate me," said Caterina. "I made you marry me when you really didn't want to."

"That's not true," said Etienne. "I don't hate you. I love you." During Etienne's tenure in the closet, Caterina had coaxed, cajoled, needled and begged. Sweet talk and angry words. Appeals to intellect and appeals to carnality. Nothing she said could lure him from the closet. At eleven o'clock she returned to the wedding celebration and found that, even without the bride and groom, it still had a full head of steam. Teary-eyed but nevertheless fetching in a little T-shirt, she told the celebrants of her plight, of the door that stood between her and marital bliss. And snicker as they might at the absurdity of the situation, not a woman there could help but feel the greatest pity for Caterina's wedding night woes. Nor could any of the men help but lament the opportunity Etienne was passing up and wish that the opportunity were his.

At Caterina's sobbing request, Etienne's father went up to talk the young man in a matter-of-fact, father-to-son, man-to-man sort of way. He spoke of honor, duty and masculinity. He explained both plumbing and methodology. He even shared some of the secrets of his own liaisons, naming several names that might have shocked Etienne were he not so wrapped up in his own turmoil.

Finally, the old man concluded his tour of duty at the closet door with some fatherly advice: "Get out of that closet and do the manly thing with your wife or I will leave everything to Hippolyte." Even this most fearsome of threats did not budge Etienne.

Caterina waited patiently among the panting, pawing paramours who now saw their own selfish overtures as sympathetic gestures that were quite honorable given the situation. When the old man returned, he just sighed and gave her a sorry look. He did not speak to her but instead found his other son. After a few words with his father,

Hippolyte climbed the stairs and took up position outside the closet door.

Figuring that his brother was either virgin or homosexual, Hippolyte crafted his remarks accordingly. He first spoke about the inherent superiority of women as sexual partners for men. Next he gave Etienne the benefit of his own proven technique. And he finished up with a highly imaginative account of what it would be like to make love to Caterina herself, being boldly descriptive considering he spoke to her husband.

He was becoming wildly innovative when the subject of his discourse appeared in the flesh, having grown weary not only of the behavior of the swains below but of the immovable object in the closet as well.

"My dear husband," said Caterina, her sweet voice not quite concealing a razor's edge. "I love you very much, but I am not going to try to persuade you from the closet any more tonight. I am going to my bed where I will be lying in all nakedness should you desire to quit the closet and do what people usually do on their wedding night. Should you choose to remain in the closet, I hope you sleep comfortably. Goodnight, Etienne. Goodnight Hippolyte."

Caterina had lain in her bed as advertised, sometime sobbing, but growing ever more relaxed and sleepy as the rum she had been drinking sang its alcoholic lullaby. Finally, just as she was about to cross over into sleep, he came to her. She started to speak, but he placed a finger to her lips, then his lips to her lips and finally all of him to all of her. The lullaby became a sweet song of love, an energetic rhapsody, and then a horns-blaring, drums-pounding, cymbals-clanging orchestral brouhaha — a crescendo punctuated by cannons and fireworks.

And then they were quiet. As Caterina slipped into slumber, her voice trailing off, she said "Oh Etienne. It was so wonderful. I never expected. If it will always require you to spend hours in the closet preparing for it, I don't care. I'll wait. I'll wait. I'll . . ." After she had slept for several minutes, Hippolyte arose, dressed quickly and returned to the party below. And to his credit, he told no one there of his adventure.

In the closet, the groom slept. And he dreamed. He dreamed of Caterina, of the two of them together. Dreams inspired by Hippolyte's description, magnified by his own desires and fancies. It was the most vivid dream he had ever had. She came to him in the closet, and they made love right there. It was like nothing he had ever known. And then she left the closet, leaving the door wide open, and said, "Come to bed, my darling. Everything is well. We'll sleep now."

And Etienne, without ever really waking, left the solitude of his closet. He went to the bedroom, lay down next to his sleeping wife, and did not move again until aroused the next morning by her kiss.

SICK IN DE STOMACH

"Albert, you're not sick," said Peaches, handing a mug of strong tea to the man lying on the chaise lounge wearing an oversized nightshirt that made him look much frailer than he actually was. Peaches, who would not reveal the source of her nickname, had by default fallen into a grudging guardianship of the cantankerous old Frenchman. "You're just imagining these things because you know you should be up on your feet being a human being."

"We have no aspirin," answered Albert. "Are we a third world country that we have no aspirin? How can a civilized people have no aspirin?"

"Because no one has been to Guadeloupe for two weeks. We're running out of things."

"It is because this island has no pharmacy," said Albert. "It is the twenty-first century. How can an island be without a pharmacy?"

"You always said pharmacies are a plague of civilization," said Peaches. "That easy access to medicine creates sick people, people dependent on medicine. That's what you said."

"I was a well man when I said that. Now I need a pharmacy because I need aspirin because I am a sick man. Is that so difficult to understand? Please speak, don't nod; my vision is blurred."

"That's because you're a cross-eyed old fool," Peaches said warmly.

"Perhaps I am, perhaps I am," Albert almost whispered. "And I'm a burden. But please don't think ill of me. I may only be a burden for another day or two. The tea is very nice. I appreciate your bringing it to me. Would you recite for me, please, the tiger poem you love so much? I'd like to hear it once more."

Peaches was dumbstruck. Albert had always criticized her love of poetry, particularly British poetry, and now he was requesting a recital. Maybe he was dying after all. What other reason could he have? He needed a pretty thought to take him to heaven. Peaches couldn't deny such a request, even if he were dreaming his illnesses, so she recited in a very serious poetic voice: "Tiger, tiger, burning bright, in the jungle late at night . . . uh . . . afraid of nothing but where they bury." She paused, then grinned and said: "For this tiger is fearful of the cemetery." Peaches had, of course, ad-libbed the final two lines, but they were quite good, capturing the spirit, if not the exact wording, of the original. She repeated it once again, giving more emphasis to the dramatic elements she had created, then sat smiling with satisfaction, waiting for Albert to voice his appreciation.

"I think the dog is probably rabid," said Albert.

"Why do you say that?"

"He bit me."

"It's a she," Peaches corrected.

SICK IN DE STOMACH

"It is my understanding that rabies is found equally among the two sexes of the species."

"Yes, but she doesn't have rabies," said Peaches. "She just doesn't like you."

"We would be able to find out for certain if there were a veterinarian on this island," Albert lamented. "But of course there isn't. There are probably a thousand veterinarians in Paris. But not here. We don't even have a doctor. This is no place to live. In France, there are specialists. If I have a heart attack here, I have no chance. If disease sweeps the island, we'll all die."

"But you said that doctors were worse than disease," Peaches reminded him. "You said the only difference between a medical doctor and a witch doctor was their makeup."

"I have said a great many things in my life."

"And now they're coming back to haunt you."

"Situations change," said Albert, sighing. "I hope you'll excuse me now. Conversation has made me weak. I must rest."

"So old Albert's a sick'un, is he?" said Basil, downing his first rum of the day. Basil had always thought himself to be a descendent of the pirate, Sir Basil Ringrose, and as each day sailed toward sunset and the rum clouded his horizon, he metamorphosed into the pirate himself.

"That's too bad," said Mutton, Basil's young protégé, whose mind was also clouded, even without the benefit of rum. "Being sick doesn't feel very good."

"Albert's only sick for one reason," Peaches declared. "Tomorrow's his birthday."

"Why would his birthday make him sick?" asked Christian, Peaches' ward and the youngest and wisest of the three men who sat with her at one of the six tables on the open pavilion that was Albert's Booby Bay Cafe.

"I don't know," said Peaches. "I guess it's because he's old and foolish, and birthday's make him feel older and more foolish. And this one's his seventieth so he's really old and really foolish."

"Old Albert ain't so foolish," said Basil, coming to his rescue, which was the proper thing to do since he was drinking Albert's rum.

"He'll get over it," said Peaches. "By Monday, he'll be himself — for better or worse."

"Seventy years," mused Basil, as he lumbered over to the bar and refreshed his rum. "Here's to old Albert bein' seventy." He took a drink. "By rights, we ought to be givin' the little frog a birthday present of some sorts."

"What do you give the man who hates everything?" asked Christian.

"A watch," suggested Mutton. The others had long since given up trying to follow Mutton's thinking.

"Where would we get a watch?" complained Christian. "We'd have to go to Guadeloupe to get a watch. We don't have time."

"If we had a watch, we'd have plenty a' time," chortled Basil.

"Besides," said Christian, not nearly as amused at Basil's joke as Basil, "he probably would hate a watch."

Basil chuckled on for a few more minutes, then said: "I know somethin' Albert don't hate." He grinned, smug in his ownership of a piece of knowledge the others lacked.

"What would that be?" asked Peaches, the only one willing to give Basil his satisfaction.

"Turtle soup," Basil pronounced. "Old Albert likes turtle soup a whole lot."

"You're right," said Christian. "I've heard him say how much he loves turtle soup."

"He loves turtle soup made in Paris," said Peaches.

"Is turtles of the French persuasion somehow different than ordinary turtles?" Basil scoffed. "A seafarin' man knows a turtle is a turtle."

"Unless it's a terrapin," said Christian with a smirk.

"Isn't that a canvas thing?" asked Mutton, looking bewildered.

"Ain't no such thing as a canvas turtle, boy," said Basil. "They'd be awful chewy."

"Turtle soup would be nice," Peaches mused.

"And medicinal," added Christian.

"But we don't know how to make turtle soup," said Peaches.

"What's to know?" said Basil. "You gets a turtle and puts him in a soup pot and cooks him up."

"We can figure it out," said Christian. "We cook the turtle in water. That makes broth. And vegetables. And bay leaves. I know bay leaves are important in soup. And Albert talks about sherry."

"Sherry be a sissy drink," said Basil.

"It goes in the soup, Basil. Albert says it complements the turtle."

"It's old Albert what oughtta compliment the turtle," said Basil.

"I don't think I've ever heard Albert compliment turtles or anything else," said Peaches, not wanting the boys to be disappointed.

"What I meant was . . ." said Christian. "Oh, never mind. This afternoon we'll go out and find all the ingredients." Mutton gave him a lost look. "The things we just talked about that go into the soup. Then tomorrow we'll start cooking, and tomorrow night, turtle soup for Albert's birthday dinner."

"Lead on, Cap'n," said Basil, and the three of them marched off, leaving Peaches with profound doubts about the soup project but unwilling to interfere with their gift to the ailing Gallic gargoyle.

"I've got a dandy soup pot and loads of vegetables — onions, carrots, potatoes," said Christian, when they reconvened at noon the next day in Albert's Booby Bay Cafe.

"I got lots of leaves," said Mutton. "I couldn't find very many in the bay, so I got a bunch from out back."

"That stuff you got there is just fine and all that," said Basil, grinning. "But it ain't turtle soup yet. Old Basil's got the turtle goods." He pulled his hand from behind his back and held before them, by its tail, a three-inch turtle.

"I don't think that will make much broth," said Christian, inspecting the turtle. "Say, isn't that little Gustave's pet turtle?"

"What kind of a pet is a turtle for a young lad? Won't fetch nothin'."

"It's too small anyway," said Christian.

"Now you didn't say nothin' 'bout how big a turtle you wanted, did ya? How much turtle d'ya need? Albert's just one little Frenchie. Okay, okay, you start cookin' them onions. Mutton, take this little critter back to Gustave, and I'll go find a big turtle, which I would've found before, if someone had only said as such." Basil made a trip to the bar for a refill, then headed off alone, the rum sloshing in his glass, mumbling as he went: "The lad won't never make a seafarer, I'll warrant, not 'til he learns how to give directions proper."

The vegetables and leaves were boiling violently in the pot of water when Basil returned two hours later, dragging a bulky burlap bag behind him. "Got us a right fine turtle here," he said. "A big'un like old Moby Dick, 'cept he was a whale and Ahab only had one leg where I got two legs, and this here's a turtle." Basil ripped open the burlap bag to reveal a 200-pound tortoise. The tortoise took one look at them and retreated into his shell.

"That's a lot of turtle," said Christian.

"First he's too little, now he's too big. You're bein' mighty picky about the size of turtles. This here one's the only other one on the whole island."

"I think these turtles are endangered," said Christian.

"I know this here turtle's endangered."

"He won't fit in the pot," argued Christian.

"He wouldn't want to anyway," said Mutton. "It's pretty hot in there."

"First, we gotta dismember 'im."

"What's dismember?" asked Mutton.

Basil shook his head. "It's just like rememberin' except, in this case, we cut him into little pieces."

"Won't that hurt?" asked Mutton.

"It would if we didn't bop him on the head first."

"Have you ever bopped a turtle on the head, Basil?" Christian asked.

"Never bopped no turtle. Bashed me a scalawag though."

"What's it like?" asked Mutton. "Does it hurt a lot?"

"Well," said Basil, "first he looks at you all twirly like, eyes wigglin.' And sometimes they just stays open and keeps wigglin' while the brains squirts outen 'is skull and flies all over tarnation."

Christian blanched.

"But it don't hurt none," Basil concluded.

Christian shook his head. "Okay, go ahead and do it. I'm going to wait over there."

"Me too," said Mutton, and he followed Christian away. Basil found a good size rock and sat down next to the tortoise.

A full hour passed before Christian shouted to Basil. "Is it done yet?"

"This pesky turtle won't stick his head out so's I can bop it."

Basil remained seated next to the tortoise for the rest of the afternoon, leaving only to refill his glass of rum every fifteen minutes or so. Christian and Mutton finally rejoined him.

"Y'know," Basil confessed, "I sort of forgot which end this turtle's head is suppose to come outten. Another thing. I got sort of hungry here smellin' that soup cookin' so I been having a few tastes now and then and y'know, it tastes sorta good. I think this here turtle's been sitting next to it so long that it kinda got some turtle taste. I'll bet if we just add a little sissy sherry, even ol' Albert'll like it."

"Turtle, you say," said Albert, taking another sip from the bowl that sat on the table in front of him. The others ringed the table, watching in anticipation.

"Caught 'im myself," said Basil, grinning.

"It tastes more like sherry with a lot of pepper in it," said Albert, forcing another sip. By the time they had added the sherry, all that remained of the soup, thanks to the prolonged boiling and Basil's frequent tasting, were a few charred leaves. Peaches had tried to perk up the bowl of hot sherry and leaves with a healthy dose of pepper. "Interesting leaves," Albert mused. "My good sherry, I suspect."

"Only the best for ol' Albert."

"I always preferred sherry in a glass, accompanied by a good cigar," said Albert. "But it's so much more delicate served hot with leaves floating in it. Perhaps you'll let me savor it in solitude. I'm afraid I might spill a precious droplet or two with everyone watching. If you'd be so good as to bring a cigar when you return."

They marched out, and when they returned five minutes later, all that remained of Albert's birthday soup was a little dampness on the lips of his satisfied smile. Only Peaches noticed the curious puddle underneath the table.

"Thank you, my friends," said Albert, lighting a cigar. "I only wish there were another bowlful, such is my appetite for turtle soup. Perhaps I'll go to Guadeloupe tomorrow."

"Here's to ol' Albert bein' seventy," said Basil, downing a glass of rum. "Happy birthday, Albert," chorused the others. Albert smiled, and Peaches was compelled to recite: "Tiger, tiger, burning bright . . ."

Coconut Woman

Harriet Forrester was no fool. For one thing, she gave no heed to Everett Limpole's bodeful warning that this stretch of beach would be completely underwater within five years — four-and-one-half feet below sea level in 1,856 days, to be exact — a prediction he reiterated after each session of poring over a loft full of books and charts, in a loft owned by Harriet for which Everett promptly paid the first of every month. Harriet Forrester was no fool.

Nor did she pay much attention to Malachi Thorpe, an Everett Limpole cohort, who had his own set of books and charts, with maps as well, but an entirely different hobbyhorse — namely, that the pirate Henri Caesar had plundered these parts and that some of his treasure lay buried and still undiscovered, possibly on this very beach. Malachi also accepted the Everett Limpole rising ocean scenario, thereby giving a certain sense of urgency to his treasure hunt. Harriet Forrester did not share either his belief in pirate treasure or his urgency. She was no fool.

Harriet did, however, have her own hobbyhorse, the Coconut House — her bed and breakfast inn, her first love, her world. It sat right on one of the prettiest beaches on the entire island against a backdrop of sea grapes and frangipani. It had, in addition to the Limpole loft, which brought in just ninety dollars a month (but steady, month in, month out), three small suites that fetched ninety dollars a night, albeit more sporadically.

Harriet's rental units had become microcosms of her own ideas, travels and interests. The Casablanca Suite revolved around its ceiling fan. Persian and Oriental rugs were scattered over a tile floor and, in some places, up the walls; fifty-four strings of bright beads served as the bathroom door; a jeweled music box played a tinny version of As Time Goes By; and portraits of Bogart, Bergman, Greenstreet, and Lorre were simply framed and grouped on one wall, looking very much like members of the family.

The New Orleans Suite was all that jazz, from a 1980's stereo flanked by a vinyl who's who of the Dixieland world to the trumpets, trombones and banjos Harriet had rescued from pawnshops and second-hand stores. And the Coconut Suite looked as though the Marx brothers had washed up during high tide.

Despite detailed literature warning what one would encounter at the Coconut House, guests would often arrive only to refuse to stay in any one of the three rooms. It didn't bother Harriet any. It was her place, and if folks didn't like it, they weren't her kind of folks anyway. And those that did stay loved it, and they came back, and they told friends who came and told other friends, and Harriet kept pretty busy.

Harriet would frequently sit with her guests on the big front porch that faced the beach. There they could talk while waves tumbled in, pelicans cruised in perfect formation inches above the water, and sandpipers darted across the sand like tiny wind-up toys. Everett Limpole would more than likely join them, and Malachi often did as well. Everett and Malachi were both there that evening in March when Harriet entertained the young couple from Ottawa, here for their fifth anniversary. As usual, Everett was explaining to the newcomers his settling-land-rising-water theory.

"Now if you was to come back for your tenth anniversary," said Everett, scratching furiously with a stubby pencil in a tiny spiral notebook, "the water'd be right up to here." He held his outstretched hand between his nose and upper lip. The young woman from Ottawa looked at him and gulped as though she were already threatened, since a water level just below Everett's nose would be well above hers.

"It's just a matter of time," Everett continued. "And not very much time at that. The forces of nature move ever and evermore onward."

"Honey, you know that can't be true," said Harriet. It wasn't clear whether honey was Everett or the young woman from Ottawa. "It's like the ozone layer and global warming and such. Scientists scribble in their little notepads just like Everett here, and they come up with statistics to prove whatever they think needs proving. Now, if I was to get up at say seven in the morning, and it was say forty degrees out, but it got up to eighty by noon, I could scribble in my little notebook and come up with a theory that by five o'clock it'd be a hundred and sixty degrees, now couldn't I?"

The young woman from Ottawa giggled a little, and her husband smiled. Everett glared, snorted and said: "It ain't that simple, and you know full well, Harriet."

"Well, maybe not," said Harriet. "But Malachi's ideas are pretty simple, aren't they Malachi? When you going to start in on them?"

"I don't know if it's something I should talk about," said Malachi, studying the couple from Ottawa.

"Why not?" asked Harriet. "You're always talking about your pirates."

"But lately I been wonderin' if maybe too many people are gettin' to know about it."

"I'd say the more people the better," Harriet teased. "If we're gonna find that treasure, honey, we got to get serious looking before it's all under water." She hee-hawed and slapped the arms of her rocker. The couple from Ottawa joined in but only with polite little laughs that wouldn't offend the two men and their theories.

"Henri Caesar was a pirate that learned his trade from the infamous Lafitte brothers," said Malachi suddenly, evidently seeing his window of opportunity swinging shut. "Cruel, cruel he was. Plundered for nearly thirty years before they hanged him. Hundreds of ships. I've studied him a lot, and I'm certain that he buried some of his treasure around here, possibly on this very beach. Half mile south of here they found an old grave. Caesar usually killed his victims, all of them, right on the ship, except certain young women he took a fancy to. If they refused his advances, he'd kill them too. But if they accepted, they were spared, at least until he grew tired of them. They found one of them in that grave. At least part of her."

The young woman from Ottawa, white-faced and wide-eyed, winced and said: "My goodness."

"And in nearly two hundred years," Harriet scoffed, "nobody has been able to find that treasure. But Malachi's going to find it before this place becomes an aquarium."

Harriet's debunking of the Malachi treasure myth was interrupted by the appearance of two men whose arrival was so silent and sudden that it caused the young woman from Ottawa to let out a tiny shriek and Harriet herself to jump slightly. They were both rumpled and shaggy, though not dirty. The tall one could have passed for a pirate and probably was in the eyes of the young woman from Ottawa. The shorter, clean-shaven one spoke in a studied, polite, but somewhat gravelly voice. "Good evening, folks. Sorry to disturb you. We've tied up at the harbor down the road for the night. Headed to the out islands tomorrow morning. Gentlemen there said you were the closest place that took in folks for the night, and we was wondering if you might have a room available."

Harriet studied the two men. She was an outgoing and trusting lady, but she was no fool, and she didn't want to get stiffed for a night's rent even if the New Orleans Suite was between guests this particular night. Nor did she want any of her semi-precious belongings spirited out during the night. As if sensing her apprehension, the shorter man produced a handful of twenty dollar bills as an unspoken offer of payment in advance, something Harriet couldn't have brought herself to ask for but was more than willing, in this particular case, to accept. "The New Orleans Suite is available this evening," she said, "Would you care to look it over. Some folks find it doesn't fit their taste."

"No need to ma'am," the man answered. "We're very tired. Won't be doing nothing but sleep and we'll be out right early." He smiled at her, eyes twinkling. "So we really don't care about ambience." He pronounced the word perfectly. "And what do you charge for your New Orleans room?"

"Ninety dollars," said Harriet. "That includes a full breakfast."

He counted out five twenties and handed them to Harriet. "Here you go. But I'm afraid we'll be skipping breakfast. We'll be leaving at the crack of dawn."

"In that case, I'll make it eighty," said Harriet, handing back a twenty.

"If you insist," said the man with another of his disarming smiles.

Harriet dug the key out of her pocket and handed it to him. " It's through that door and to the right. Hope you have a pleasant sleep."

"I'm sure we will," said the shorter man turning. The other man smiled for the first time as he turned to follow his partner. He was missing a tooth.

Harriet, sensing that the young couple were uneasy about sleeping under the same roof with the two strangers — the young woman was, in fact, certain they'd all be murdered in their sleep — said: "We get a lot of sailors and fishermen here. They pretty much keep to themselves. You know, aloof. But if you ever get them talking, well honey, they can really spin some stories. Too bad they're not staying for breakfast. You'd get a pretty good picture about this part of the world."

Harriet's cheerfulness calmed the young couple and a few moments later they sought the privacy of their room to do fifth anniversary things. Malachi finished his beer and headed off down the road to his own apartment over Gunny's Restaurant. Everett scribbled in his spiral notebook for a while, then made for his loft, where he would probably punch numbers into his pocket calculator for a good hour before going to sleep. Harriet mixed a batch of muffin dough, refrigerated it, and returned to the porch where she sat staring at the starry sky and swaying with the steady lapping of the surf. She loved this porch; she loved this place. She realized sitting here that this place was more important than any silly pirate treasure, even if she believed in such a thing, which she didn't. Finally, she reluctantly quit the porch and went upstairs to bed.

She slept in spurts. More than once she thought she heard noises above the natural rhythm of the night but when she listened carefully, even sitting right up once, she heard nothing, and she went back to sleep. Asleep, she dreamed about the man with the missing tooth. He was carrying water up the beach and pouring it on her porch. And then there were two of him, four of him, eight of him, just like the brooms in Fantasia. The water was up to her knees when she woke up to sunshine.

She shuddered at the nightmare, dressed quickly and hurried to the New Orleans Suite. The men were gone, and the only mementos of their stay were an empty whiskey bottle in the garbage can and a Fats Waller record out of its jacket on the floor in front of the stereo. Otherwise the room was perfect; they had even made the bed. She went back to the kitchen, poured herself a glass of half tomato juice half Bloody Mary mix, put the coffee on, beat ten eggs, and whipped up some Hollandaise sauce, all the while singing it's still the same old story, a fight for love and glory, a case of do or die; the fundamental things apply, as time goes by.

Breakfast preparation complete, she walked around to the front of the house, picked up the newspaper and headed for her spot on the porch to wait for her guests to arise. What she found on the porch was not her favorite chair; that had been tossed into the hibiscus bush. What she found were weathered boards strewn for ten feet around a yawning hole in the ground where her porch had been the night before. She stared into the hole in disbelief. At the bottom of the whole, she spotted indentations in the dirt suggesting that something heavy and rectangular had been sitting down there.

Then she spotted a coin at the edge of the hole. She reached down and picked it up. It was gold, and it had Spanish words engraved on it. She stared back at the hole then studied the coin again. Laughing, she said aloud: "Poor, poor Malachi. He won't be a happy man."

She pushed the coin into her pocket and went inside. After calling the carpenter, she returned to the kitchen where she put the muffins in the oven and wondered, just briefly, if the floorboards beneath her weren't a little spongier than usual.

All Day, All Night, Marianne

Toussaint conned his small motorboat to the empty spot at the pier, near where Roberto lolled, dangling his big bare feet in the warm water. The boat, like Toussaint's shirt and shorts, had the scars of a life well lived. On each side, the hand-lettered word taxi just above the waterline made it an official vehicle for transporting passengers up, down, and around the island's seven-mile coastline.

Toussaint nodded and took up a cross-legged position next to Roberto.

Roberto grunted in reply.

"What's the matter?" asked Toussaint.

"Nothing," answered Roberto in a child's whine, the kind that begs for additional prodding. "Nothing. I was at Pigeon Beach today."

Toussaint sighed. "Man, you gotta get over this."

"I can't. She's just so beautiful. She was there playing with the children again. And again she didn't even see me. When she looked in my direction, it was like I wasn't even standing there. She just looked through me like I was invisible, a ghost or something. Perhaps if she wasn't so beautiful, she could see me."

"Perhaps," said Toussaint, turning it over in his mind. "But if she could see you, maybe she would see you ugly."

"I'm not so ugly."

"Of course not," said Toussaint with a reassuring grin. "But you're no Jean Paul either." Jean Paul was the young man held up as an example of what young manhood was all about. The other men didn't like him much – he was so knowledgeable and so arrogant – but they had to grudgingly agree that he was the handsomest of them all. And he paraded his handsomeness and pursued all the young women on the island, even many of the tourists. His only notable failure was with Marianne, Roberto's young woman at Pigeon Beach, and this gave Roberto some small satisfaction. But as Toussaint tactfully pointed out, if Jean Paul couldn't win Marianne, what possible chance could Roberto have?

"You should say something to her," Toussaint argued. "You can't expect her to pay you no mind, standing there like the ghost of Albert Verra." In island history, Albert Verra had the dubious distinction of being the ultimate coward, selling out his island once to the French and once to the Spanish.

"I try, but I am afraid."

"Maybe I have an idea for you, Roberto," said Toussaint, lowering his voice even though there was no one within thirty yards of the pier. "You know the fine gentleman from that city I can't remember that's very close to London, the one who takes my water taxi wherever he goes and pays me very generously? Him and me, we're friends now. He talks to me about all sorts of things. He's very educated in literacy – that's reading important books by dead people and looking at pictures and listening to music, all by dead people. It seems people who write books and paint pictures and make music become important when they die."

"What good is being important if you're dead? Doesn't sound all that educated to me."

"How would you know educated, man?" said Toussaint, just a little miffed at Roberto's effrontery in questioning him. "His name is Herbert and he's got two last names. Now, do you want me to help you, or do you want to spend your life on the beach staring at her with your mouth open and your brain shut until you both get old and die?"

"I want you to help me," said the chastened Roberto. He stared at his feet as he swirled them in the water.

"Okay," said Toussaint, once again in command. "Now, Herbert was telling me this very, very famous story by a guy that's been dead for close onto 400 years. Four hundred – now that makes him mighty important. The guy in the story is like you. His name is Romeo; that even sort of sounds like Roberto. This Romeo, he loves a girl whose name I forget. It doesn't sound like Marianne, but I guess that doesn't matter. Julianne, that's it. I guess it sounds a

little like Marianne. Now Julianne's family don't like Romeo
one little bit."

"Why doesn't her family like him?" asked Roberto
whose face now showed only confusion.

"Because Julianne is very beautiful, just like
Marianne, but Romeo has this great big nose. So Romeo
sneaks to Julianne's back porch every night and hides in the
bushes and says pretty words while her big fat mama sleeps
inside. He says things like, 'Julianne, my sweetest sweet,
your face is like the moon.' And Julianne says, 'Oh Romeo,
I can't see your face; it's behind the bushes. Show me your
face.' And Romeo says, 'No, no, fair princess. I cannot.
But it's a nice face – with a tiny nose.' And Julianne says,
'Romeo, Romeo, wherefore are you, Romeo?' See how they
use each other's names a lot? That's very romantic."

"Wherefore?"

"That's 400-year-old talk. But this is what puts
smart dudes like me and Herbert over here and dumb dudes
like you over on the beach with your mouth open and bugs
flying in and out. When Julianne says wherefore, she isn't
wondering where Romeo is."

"No?"

"Of course not. She knows he's in the bushes. What she's really saying is why. Herbert explained that to me."

"Why?"

"Because him and me is friends."

"No, I mean why is wherefore 'why'? And why would she ask Romeo why he is Romeo?"

"Because it's literacy," said Toussaint, trying his best not to patronize poor Roberto. "She wants to know why it has to be Romeo out there instead of someone else."

"How come?"

"Because he has such a big nose, of course."

Roberto thought about this story for a moment, kicking at the water with one foot and then the other. Toussaint studied him, looking for some sign that maybe he understood.

"Why doesn't she just tell him to go away?" asked Roberto finally.

Toussaint grinned. "Because she loves all the pretty words he says to her. And before long, she loves him, too — nose and all. And all because he talked pretty. As Herbert says, the story don't end until the fat lady sings."

"What?"

"The fat lady. I guess at the end of all these famous stories a fat lady sings. That's how you know it's over. So all you got to do, Roberto, is hide outside Marianne's porch and say pretty words and hope she falls in love with you before a fat lady sings."

"But I don't know any pretty words," Roberto whined.

"I'll help you find some pretty words. It's easy the songs on the jukebox at the Crab Hole are just filled with pretty words."

Later that morning, Toussaint delivered Herbert Trent-Phillips to a social gathering at the tip of the island, earning in the process the twenty dollars that was to pay for their research at the Crab Hole that afternoon. The Crab Hole was aptly named, except that no self-respecting crab would make a home in this particular hole. Its four rickety tables were generally filled by the water-taxi drivers during the afternoon lull when the French tourists drank wine and insulted each other, the British took tea in the shade, and pasty Americans tried to erase generations of hereditary white skin in an orgiastic bout with the Caribbean sun. The rum was cheap, and the vintage tunes on the Crab Hole's jukebox even cheaper. Toussaint's twenty dollars was split sixty-forty between rum and golden oldies, and the two young men spent the afternoon soaking up both. Roberto mostly sat and sipped his courage, for Toussaint was not about to let another day go by before his literacy brought these two starfish-crossed lovers together whether they liked it or not; Roberto would give his performance that very night at Marianne's back porch. Toussaint himself scribbled on a paper placemat as the seductive words of Johnny Cash, Fats Domino, and the Purple People Eater filled the Crab Hole air. Roberto's declaration of love was completed by 5 o'clock, and from then until dusk, Toussaint put him through a rigorous dress rehearsal.

The sun took its evening dip in the placid Caribbean. With a sense of adventure amplified by alcohol and the growing belief that they had entered a new literary realm in which Toussaint, Roberto, and Herbert Trent-Phillips were the only living souls, pledges in the fraternity of immortality, and not unhappy to remain pledges if the price of full membership were death, they pointed Toussaint's aquatic hack toward Palmas Bay, where

Marianne and her mother lived, if you can call a life without Toussaint and Roberto in it living.

Roberto would find Marianne's dwelling romance-friendly, for it had not just a back porch but an actual balcony in the Shakespearean sense, one that might have been designed for the delivering of soliloquies. And actually it had been designed that way, or at least as a romantic place to stare at the moon and breathe bosomy sighs, for Marianne's mother had been a dramatis persona of sorts in her younger days. But that was three husbands, forty years, and 200 pounds ago.

Roberto and his speechwriter crept through the fragrant frangipani up to the back of the house. Toussaint remained at a short distance so he could see everything, but pushed Roberto ahead to where nature in her cooperative way had placed a pretty hibiscus, just the right size and shape for concealing a swain and his cue cards.

"Marianne," whispered Roberto in a voice not unlike the wicked witch of the west's. No answer.

"Marianne," he said louder, his voice cracking but at least without menace in it. The fact that the earth had not opened up and swallowed him gave Roberto a little lift, and he said more assertively and louder still: "Oh, dear one."

When he heard movement on the balcony above, he pointed the little flashlight at Toussaint's script and cleared his throat. Toussaint did not hear the creaking of the balcony, but he saw the appearance of the very large shadowy figure. He tried frantically to signal Roberto, but Roberto was staring at his script and reciting his words of love:

"Oh, petite flower, you make the moon stand still, because you're such a thrill, you're my blueberry hill . . ."

At the first words, the woman on the balcony started and began to retreat through the door. But then she stopped, returned to the edge of the balcony and looked down, searching the shadows below for a sign of the intruder.

"I walk the line over you, baby, baby, because you are my sunshine, my only sunshine, even though right now it's only moonshine . . ."

She still watched, but now she was content to listen a bit longer to the words coming to her from out of the darkness.

"Hold me close, hold me tight, make me scream all the night. I don't only have eyes for you. I have lips and arms and a nose – but just a little one – for you. With all these things I have, I want to caress you . . ."

The woman on the balcony swayed to the sounds below, and the balcony creaked even more, so Roberto was forced to speak even louder.

"I want to squeeze you like a snake, pinch you like a crab. You'll never know, dear, how much I love you and want to touch you . . ." Roberto heard heavy breathing from above, and although it sounded very heavy indeed for his diminutive Marianne, he guessed that his words were affecting her deeply, so much so that he skipped ahead a few lines to the good stuff.

"I want to touch you all over. Put my lips to your sweet . . ."

Toussaint was to him now, shaking him, whispering urgently, "It's not Marianne."

"Lips," Roberto continued before fully understanding what Toussaint was saying.

Upon understanding the error, Roberto wanted so desperately to sneak away, to try another day, but the little hibiscus that was his concealment had become a prison as well. Now the balcony was quaking in earnest, and a thunderous soprano voiced pierced the tropical night with its melody:

"Take my hand, you little stranger in paradise . . ."

Roberto knew full well the import of that singing – it was too late for him and Marianne. If only he could escape with what little dignity a wretch such as he could have.

Having sung, the fat lady concentrated on coaxing her bashful secret admirer from his sanctuary: "Wherefore art thou, my little cupcake. Come out, come out, whereforever thou art."

Toussaint was about to smugly point out the mistaken usage by the siren on the balcony when Roberto turned as white as a 400-year-old poet. Marianne had joined her mother on the balcony and together they were scanning the shrubbery for signs of Mama's plucky paramour.

"Oh, don't let her see me," Roberto pleaded. "Make me invisible so she won't see me."

"If you don't come out, I'll come find you, naughty boy," said Marianne's mama as Marianne tried unsuccessfully to contain her laughter. In mortal fear of being identified as Mama's Romeo, Roberto seized

Toussaint and, with the strength of ten Robertos, hurled him into the open courtyard.

"There you are, my speckled bird," cooed Marianne's mama. Toussaint stood and grinned. "Wait right there, sweet boy. Your blueberry hill is coming for you." Roberto watched from the hibiscus, and Marianne from the balcony, as Mama appeared in the courtyard and chased poor Toussaint into the darkness.

Roberto stared up at Marianne, as lovely on the balcony a she was on the beach, and suddenly words of his very own creation poured forth as effortlessly as if he were pantomiming to someone else's speech: "All day, all night, Marianne . . ." And he stepped out from behind the hibiscus into full view of the balcony. "Down by the seashore sifting sand."

"Aren't you the one from the beach?" asked Marianne. "I've seen you many times, but you seemed not to see me."

Let a hundred — no, a thousand — fat ladies sing, thought Roberto, as his words of love for Marianne continued to tumble forth.

MAMA EU QUERO

The flickering image on the T-V screen – strong
eyes, the familiar beard, the damn fatigue cap – stole Delia's
attention from the book she had determined to finish this
evening. And his voice – still defiant, but the words he
uttered were words of defeat, stepping down. *All these years,
and your revolution will end with a whimper. I'm afraid it's getting
old and wrinkled, Fidel. Like us.*

The face on the TV screen changed,
metamorphosing into another image from the distant past

that probably wasn't really there. It was a gentler face with a mischievous smile and a great big nose, a face that forced both a smile and a tear as he cooed: "Good night Mrs. Calabash, wherever you are." It was an odd association, these two faces, but for Delia, lasting and inevitable. Jimmy Durante disappeared into the darkness and Fidel was back.

Delia didn't hate Fidel the way so many of the others she knew who had had associations with Cuba did. Of course her association with Cuba had been very short – but intense – a mere two months during that bittersweet summer of 1955, three and a half years before Castro took power. She was a young woman – a girl – plucked from the American Midwest by a tornado and whisked into a wild and wicked Oz called Havana. There to meet Jorge. And Maria do Carmo Miranda da Cunha.

Maria do Carmo Miranda da Cunha was not born in Brazil as many think. She emigrated from Portugal, arriving in Rio de Janeiro in 1910. But once there, she so fully absorbed the culture of her new home that she would one day personify its people, its infectious rhythms. On the world stage and in the many movies that, years later, Delia would watch on television, Carmen Miranda was Brazil.

By today's reckoning, the revolution was already two years underway that summer Delia's father got an assignment with an American sugar company in Havana. In a way, by working for a sugar company with vast interests in Cuba, her father and by extension his family, including Delia, were in their own small way partially responsible for the revolution. Sugar (Delia still couldn't put it in her coffee) was both Cuba's lifeblood and its yoke. A third of the country's income depended on sugar, and American sugar companies controlled three-fourths of the land on which it could be grown. And the entire blame, at least in Delia's eyes, seemed to have fallen on one sixteen-year-old girl.

When Maria do Carmo Miranda da Cunha was sixteen, she was already an entertainer in her own small part of the world. She quickly became known in her own country, and in 1939, as Carmen Miranda, she sambaed to the United States for a part in a Broadway musical review. The tower of fruit above the slight five-foot-one Brazilian

Bombshell became an instant trademark, which along with her musical exuberance carried her to super stardom. She appeared in many films, but Delia's favorite was an outrageous Busby Berkeley musical in which she sang "The Lady with the Tutti Frutti Hat" while an army of dancers waved giant bananas. Why would a young teenager idolize Carmen Miranda when the other girls her age wished to be Marilyn Monroe or Rita Hayworth or Grace Kelly? Perhaps it was because even though Carmen wasn't so pretty, she was so vital. And they said she was really very shy. Just like Delia.

Jorge's last words to her were: "We'll be together soon, I promise." His first words had been: "Another *Norteamericano*. Would you like me to lie on the floor so you can walk on me?" She had cried both times. His last words echoed for many months even as she realized that although they were probably truthful in intent, they were spoken in summer, in Cuba, and in youth. Jorge's first words were quickly forgotten. They burned, made her feel a guilt that should not have been hers. But even though his words were mean and insensitive, Jorge was not, and as soon as he had uttered them, he felt shame at having hurt a person who had done him no harm, at having acted in the same manner as those he criticized. Spurred by her tears, his apologies rushed forth. And within five minutes they were sharing their first Cuban beer, their first conversation and the first day of a summer idyll that would careen through the hot weeks of June and July like a possessed Cuban taxi on an open road.

Many of those conversations would turn to politics, and Delia showed a naiveté about the affairs of the country that stood just 90 miles from her own country's doorstep. At the center of such conversations stood Fulgencio Batista y Zaldivar, and Jorge would loudly decry his infamy. "Fulgencio cares only for Fulgencio," he would snort. When on a soapbox, he always used Batista's given name. "He doesn't give a damn for the people. They hate him, too. And he knows it. But he has the army and the police, so he doesn't need the people. Let me tell you how the great Fulgencio cares for his people. Two years ago, Fidel's attempt at revolution was put down almost as quickly as it started. The gunfire that we could hear off and on through Saturday night had died down by Sunday morning, and my father insisted we go to church as usual. During the service, the police appeared at all entrances to the church, blocking our exit except through the one door that opened onto the square. Just in front of that door, close enough so that we must negotiate around it, the police had dumped a wagonload of bloodied bodies. As we passed by we could see movement within this noxious heap and hear low groans. Some of them had not yet died."

Jorge turned his face away from Delia as the tears appeared in his eyes. She shuddered and cried with him. What seemed to bother him the most was the hopelessness. The people grumbled and cursed, but they were apathetic. The opposition made speeches, but they were meaningless; when in power, the opposition had been corrupt too. Fidel had been released from prison but was in exile.

As deep as Jorge's anger was, Delia conquered and subdued it as their relationship grew. And for a time his country's turmoil became as distant to him as Ike and Iowa were to her.

To Delia's father, what was happening at home was infinitely more important than what was happening here in Cuba. As a result Cuban papers rarely found their way into the household. The New York Times did, however, although by the time it arrived the news was as cold as a Manhattan January. Nevertheless it served the noble purpose of convincing him that he had not fallen off the edge of civilization. And it was from this unlikely source that Delia learned the fantastic news.

She and Jorge had, just a day earlier, shared their first kiss. It was an awkward moment during which each of them was so concerned about the other's reaction that the end result rivaled the emotional wallop of a two-cheek greeting from a forgotten aunt. But later – for Delia anyway, when she was alone – that anemic kiss blossomed into the most lyrical and sensual act of all time, superior to any kiss any time anywhere by any couple, living or dead, including even that kiss she had witnessed through the rear view mirror of Johnny Edward's '49 Ford, a kiss involving arms and legs as much as lips. At that time, she had realized what the real difference between the sexes was; now she knew why.

And even with the passage of time, a whole 24 hours of it, she was still giddy, certain she would swoon unless she diverted her attention. So she picked up The New York Times just to let its sophisticated but utterly meaningless words ricochet off her occupied mind. And she certainly found news fit to print – just a few sentences – not about Eisenhower or Khrushchev or DeGaulle, but about Carmen Miranda. Carmen Miranda was coming to Havana to appear at the Tropicana.

Although none would ever equal in her mind that fumbling first kiss, their kisses were now accelerating in frequency and intensity. They were no longer awkward, though sometimes clumsy, perhaps, in a frenzied sort of way. She and Jorge had whizzed past everything Delia had learned from the rear view mirror and were speeding down a highway she'd never traveled before, without the aid of a road map – or if there were a road map, it was all in Spanish. Delia, however, set the speed limit and enforced it as necessary. This she usually did by breaking into conversation.

"We must go to see Carmen Miranda," Delia insisted as Jorge tried to calm himself.

"That place represents all that is wrong with Cuba," answered Jorge.

"I don't think one little nightclub can represent so much."

"It's not little."

"But it's her, Jorge. She doesn't hurt Cuba. She loves Cuba. She loves everyone. Please, Jorge."

"We'll see."

"Absolutely not," said her father.

If the Tropicana represented for Jorge all that was wrong with Cuba, it represented for her father all that was wrong with civilization. To him, the Tropicana was Sodom itself with Gomorra thrown in for good measure, and any young woman who ventured therein would be, or should be, turned to a pillar of salt or stoned by people without sin or tossed into a lion's den. (Delia knew most of the Bible stories, but she did have a little problem with proper juxtaposition.) To Delia, the Tropicana was the Promised Land, Eden, or to edge comfortably away from the Biblical, Xanadu. Once a vast private estate, it was now Cuba's most luxurious club, a place where partying parishioners went to worship the nightlife under starry Cuban skies.

"They drink there and they gamble there," her father went on. "God only knows what else they do. It's not the proper atmosphere for a child."

"I'm not a child."

"Nevertheless, you're not 21, the legal age for entering such an establishment." Delia wanted to point out that this was Havana not Dubuque, that they were probably a lot looser about such things here, but decided it would not help her cause.

"But if I can look 21and I don't drink or gamble or do anything but watch one show, what can it hurt," she pleaded.

"It would be breaking the law," said her father. This was not just a convenient parental ploy; Delia's father obeyed laws, even speed limits. "We are guests in a foreign country and it is incumbent upon us to respect that country's laws." For all Delia knew, twelve-year-olds could legally enter the Tropicana, but even if they could, she'd never convince her father it was so. She had but one recourse – deceit.

Fortune had taken a keen interest in Delia's affairs during this Cuban summer, watching over her and acting on her behalf, so it didn't surprise Delia at all when her father told her that he had to go to Santa Clara for several days, leaving just a day before Carmen Miranda arrived. Delia would be left in the care of their housekeeper Josefina, a wonderful woman who could not be distracted from her television set after nine o'clock by anything on this earth, let alone by a teenager slipping out the back door for an evening at the Tropicana.

Carmen Miranda arrived in Havana on the fourth of July in the glorious summer of 1955. There were fireworks aplenty in that nation to the north, but none here where they should have been. The previous night, with Jorge still fence sitting on the subject of taking her to the Tropicana, Delia decided to play Carmen for him, hoping this would propel him in the proper direction. She first got the idea of dressing up as Carmen Miranda after seeing the movie Scared Stiff, in which Jerry Lewis had done the same thing. Practically everyone had at some time impersonated Carmen – she was an easy study – but for Delia this particular performance was like an insurance policy: No matter how bizarre her own performance might be, it couldn't be as outlandish as this one.

She donned a costume of red, gold, orange and yellow silk scarves pinned together along with a crown of bananas, put a recording of "Cuanta la Gusta" on the player and strutted before Jorge. As the energy from the recording infused Delia, she moved with sensual abandon before her awestruck audience, their eyes locked. As the song ended, and she flew into Jorge's arms, she knew that the speed limit would be broken tonight.

The Tropicana was a frenzied, pulsating place, as animated as the tourists and Havana socialites who crowded the casino, bar, dance floor and every table, there to be entertained by a half dozen celebrities, three full orchestras and the Tropicana's own ballet troupe. It had not been easy for Jorge to secure a table, and when he did, it was some distance from where Carmen Miranda would shortly perform. He liked the table just fine, not wanting to be conspicuous in such a place. Delia wished they were closer but couldn't say anything, and just being here was the high point in her sixteen years plus four months. She looked as mature as any seventeen-year-old in the place, sipping the wine Jorge had bought her and wearing another bright outfit that Carmen herself might have worn, but without the tutti frutti hat, of course, for that would be presumptuous.

Miranda's Boys broke into a spirited overture, and suddenly there was Carmen Miranda herself, bouncing to the beat of "South American Way." Jorge turned to see the look on Delia's face, but there was no look on Delia's face because there was no Delia. He scanned the floor, fearing she had fainted in her excitement. Nothing. Then he spotted her, crawling on hands and knees between the tables, toward the stage. He closed his eyes afraid to watch but finally had to look again. He spotted her as she squeezed unnoticed between the chairs occupied by the sleek black-haired man and his sleek black-haired companion, disappearing under the table next to where - Carmen Miranda sang and danced.

Then Carmen jumped into one of Delia's favorites: "Mama mama mama eu quero, mama eu quero, mama eu quero mama, da a chupeta, da a chupeta . . ." A few lines into the song, one of her most famous and one she had probably sung hundreds of times, she stopped and stared into the immense room before her as though she had become lost. "Para bebe" came a whisper from under the nearest table. Carmen dove back into the song, and few in the audience were aware of the lapse. There were no further lapses and the song appeared to be headed toward a successful conclusion.

About the only warning the black-haired couple had of the impending disaster was the   dancing of the olives in their martinis, a nervous samba in time to the music coming from the stage. It was gentle enough at first, but then the table that gave cadence to the martinis above and shelter to the young lady below shook as energetically as a table at a three-ghost séance. Delia was out of control. Carmen Miranda finished her song, the audience roared its approval and Delia jumped to her feet, sending the table and its occupants reeling backward into yet another table and another couple like so many genteel but helpless dominoes.

The room hushed as waiters bobbed here and there to repair the damage. Two large men left their posts at a doorway and headed toward Delia. So did Carmen Miranda, who reached her first and stared at her without speaking. The Brazilian Bombshell was a little older, a little heavier than the Carmen of Delia's memory, but her brilliant eyes flashed – with anger, Delia thought. But then she grinned and said: "Zank you. You are boodifool."

She kissed Delia's forehead, darted back to the stage and resumed singing as though she were trying to divert attention from the embarrassed young woman now being escorted away from the stage.

Even now, forty years later, observed only by Fidel, Delia's cheeks reddened at the   recollection of her calamitous faux pas, a Cuban crisis every bit as important to Delia as the Bay of Pigs invasion years later. Jorge had interceded that night and Delia was allowed to return to her table for the rest of the performance. But she was watched carefully and escorted out as soon as Carmen finished.

Summer ended as abruptly as Carmen's performance of "Mama Eu Quero" when her father was summoned back to the United States in late July. And although Delia had known from the beginning that her summer would end too soon, this shortening of it was somehow unjust, and she said so over and over, but to no avail. For she and Jorge, that last day together equaled any sweet sorrow of parting ever committed by a romantic to paper, film or television screen. It was filled with lovemaking, tears and promises – promises to write or phone, to return, to visit, to never forget – all that stuff that tries but can't take the sting out of the word good-by.

In the plane, somewhere over the Gulf of Mexico, Delia heard the words to a popular song:

. . .though other nights and other days will find us gone our separate ways, we will have these moments to remember.

And she knew, despite trying all she could to believe otherwise, that Jorge and the past two months would be memories and nothing else.

The last few days of July and the first few in August were endless hours of agony. Her young life had ceased, after sixteen and a half short years, to have meaning. She mostly listened to music – Latin and melancholy – and stared at the television set, not really watching. Not until that night when Jimmy Durante had as his special guest, straight from her triumphant Cuban tour, Carmen Miranda.

Delia, cheered for the first time since leaving Cuba, even doffed a hat of fruit as she sat cross-legged in front of the television, watching the interplay between Jimmy and Carmen. Delia may have been watching with 20 million other Americans, but only she a few short weeks ago had seen Carmen Miranda from underneath a table at the Tropicana, had been smiled at and called *boodiful.*

After the lights had dimmed at the Club Durant and the star of the show had bade goodnight to Mrs. Calabash,

Carmen Miranda returned to her dressing room. There, shortly after midnight, at 46 years of age, she died of a heart attack.

Ah, look what you've done, Fidel. I hadn't thought about that summer in a good long time. For a few months, I thought of nothing else; for a few years, often. For several Halloweens, I shamelessly dressed my daughter as Carmen. And for one Halloween, her little brother was you, Fidel. Delia laughed. The face on the television screen was now a stranger, but she continued to talk to it. *Several years ago, we all watched that old movie on TV, and they laughed when I cried at the giant bananas. My husband says I should visit Cuba, but I don't think that's allowed. All because of my international incident at the Tropicana, probably. I hear the Tropicana is still there. I thought they would have torn it down at once. Jorge would have.*   *Jorge.*

Good night, Jorge, wherever you are.

JUDY DROWNDED

Leland Armbrewster saw opportunity where others saw mere misfortune.

"Hurry, Raymond," urged the young woman, skipping through the palms and sea grapes that separated the quiet beach from the laughter and tinny music spewing from the Crab Hole.

"It's too late, Judy," whined Raymond, padding behind. "It's almost midnight, and we shouldn't be here." The rhythmic lapping of the water now overpowered the scratchy wail of "Cherry Pink and Apple Blossom White," a recording that was celebrating its fiftieth year on the Crab Hole juke box.

"But this is the best time," Judy gushed. "Smell the frangipani. Look at all those stars. Look at me. She tugged at Raymond's arm, dragging him to where the water lapped at their feet. "You know why it's the best time?" She swayed back and forth, smiling at him, stupefying him with wanton eyes.

"Why?" asked Raymond.

"Because we don't have to wear anything. And you'll be able to see what all the others would die to see." She unbuttoned buttons and untied ties, letting each of her few bits of apparel drop to the sandy beach. Raymond did the same, reluctant out of fear but hooked by desire. Judy finished undressing, and Raymond, pants off, shirt still on, stared at her, unable to move. She stood, letting him stare at her momentarily, then giggled, grabbed his pants and ran into the water.

"Come and get them," she taunted. "Come and get me."

"But . . ."

"I'm waiting." Her voice had grown smaller.

"I can't swim," Raymond groaned.

"Don't be silly." Judy's voice was now as far off as "Cherry Pink and Apple Blossom White." Raymond waded into the water, until it was above his waist and tugging him toward the deep end of the ocean. He realized it was hopeless; he dared go no further, no matter how much desire percolated within him. As he retreated, he heard the distant scream – Judy's scream – just once, then silence.

"Judy," he shouted. "Are you all right?" No reply. He called her name again several times, and when there was still no answer, he turned and ran. He scrambled across the beach, back through the palms and sea grapes, tripping often, to the road and to the Crab Hole, where "Cherry Pink and Apple Blossom" bleated a final musical orgasm. He crashed through the door. The six patrons inside grabbed their glasses of rum and looked up in surprise, the now silent the jukebox heightening the drama of the moment.

"Something's happened," Raymond shouted into the silence. "Something terrible."

"Boy," said Chicken Avery. "Do you know you got no pants on?"

The people of Soleil are not hardhearted; but now and again, someone did drown. It was sad but inevitable, being surrounded by ocean. Judy had no family beyond a drunken uncle, but she was popular with the young men of the island, and it was they who grieved the most. It was taken for granted that she had drowned. In other places, they might drag a body of water for a body just to be sure, but you couldn't drag the ocean. And the ocean generally cooperated by delivering a drowned body to the beach in a timely manner. So the people expressed their remorse, got on about their lives and waited for the ocean to bring closure. But this time the ocean did not cooperate. Days passed, weeks passed, and no Judy.

The eclectic mix of music on the Crab Hole jukebox included several Hank Williams songs. In addition to being classic country recordings, the Hank Williams songs, particularly "You're Cheating Heart" and "Poor Old Kewliga," were bellwethers, unfailing signals that it was time to cut off Chicken Avery's rum. When Chicken started singing along with Hank, it was pretty much a given that he would pick a fight when the song ended unless sent home.

Thus it was that Chicken was stumbling along the beach, wailing about that brokenhearted Indian, Kewliga, adding a haphazard calypso lilt to the tune, that night in late July. As he walked, he saw something out there in the water, something staring at him with burning eyes, something large and fearsome. And he remembered Judy, who had last been seen on this very beach, whose body had never come back, because it was eaten by a shark, or something worse. He tried to run, stumbling and falling, certain the great unnamed beast was pursuing him. He could feel its hot breath, and he knew that, if he were eaten, he would be swallowed whole, not chewed.

Leland Armbrewster treasured his late evening stroll through the stillness of his beach. It wasn't Leland's beach in any legal sense; it belonged at any given moment to whoever wished to take advantage of it. But Leland's comfortable home hovered over a portion of it, and Leland was used to considering most things he surveyed to be his. In fact, it may have been that attitude that brought him to Soleil from a small town in upstate New York where, as Mayor, he took a rather proprietary interest in the town treasury, finally embezzling, to use a harsh word, a substantial golden retirement parachute. After stops in Jamaica, Barbados, and Martinique always cut short by a most doglike private investigator hired by his former townsfolk, Leland arrived in Soleil, where he now engaged in the aforementioned late evening stroll.

Leland was remarking to himself, as he did during every evening stroll, how refreshing the breeze off the water was, when a madman babbling about demons came screaming out of the dark and fell at his feet. The man held tight to Leland Armbrewster's ankles and prayed an unintelligible prayer over and over until Leland shook him loose.

The second mate of the SS Love Nest said to the third mate, as he dimmed the spotlight they had been training on the island in the distance: "That's Soleil; it's worth skipping."

Sipping a glass of Leland Armbrewster's rum, Chicken Avery jabbered on – a one-man Tower of Babel – choosing to begin his narrative at about six o'clock that evening. By the time Chicken had reached 7 p.m., Leland's mind had wandered away to more productive places, not to return until jerked back into the here and now by the words "giant beast".

Since arriving on Soleil, Leland had been looking for the best way to exploit his new home, a way to goose the tourist trade, to put the little island on yearning travelers' wish lists and, in the process, put additional wealth in Leland's yearning pockets. He had tried on one occasion to sell the island as a buccaneer's haven. He even had a local drunk who thought he was a descendent of the infamous pirate, Basil Ringrose, and who, during his rum-clouded afternoons and evenings, thought himself a true pirate. Leland discovered that tourists really don't like pirate havens, particularly when populated by pirates or would-be pirates given to inappropriate swashbuckling. And his scheme came to a premature climax when his pirate poked the wife of a visiting Legionnaire in the hiney with a cutlass.

Upon hearing "giant beast coming out of the water after me," Leland thought Loch Ness, monster aficionados and Yankee dollars. "Tell me about this giant beast," he said, pouring Chicken more rum.

This much rum, following Hank Williams, would have made Chicken himself a beast under normal circumstances. But these were not normal circumstances, and Chicken was small and scared. "It was a gigantic, horrible beast," said Chicken, not far enough gone to miss the Pavlovian link between his story and Leland's rum. And the look of interest on Leland's face encouraged him even further. "It ate Judy, poor young girl, barely eighteen, gobbled her, tried to gobble me."

"Hmmm," said Leland.

"Tried to gobble me, but I doan let it get me. Woulda swallowed me whole, but I run away."

"Hmmm," said Leland. "Tell me more about what it looked like."

"Terrible, terrible," said Chicken, staring at the ceiling as though he were trying to picture it more clearly.

"Did it have a long neck?" prompted Leland.

"Oh yes," said Chicken, shaking his head. "A long neck; a long, fat neck."

"Did it have long, spiky teeth?"

"Oh, it did. It sure did. Teeth as long and sharp as machetes."

"Did it look prehistoric?"

"Prehistoric," Chicken mumbled, then lighting up said: "Like dinosaurs. Yes sir, it looked like a great big mean water dinosaur. And it breathed fire."

"Are you sure about that?" said Leland, his stern look telling Chicken he had gone too far.

"No, I guess maybe not," Chicken answered. "Maybe not fire. But it sure did have the most hottest breath I ever felt.

"Well," said Leland, capping the rum bottle. "I think we better let the others know about this. We certainly wouldn't want this creature eating any more young girls or anyone else for that matter."

"No sir," said Chicken. "We sure doan want that."

What is this creature lurking beneath the tranquil waters of Booby Bay? asked Leland Armbrewster's press release. *A mutant from atomic testing in the fifties? A Jurassic or Pleistocene leftover? Does it matter? To those few who have seen this beast, it is an awesome example of evolutionary grandeur.*

The catamaran whined as the tenth octogenarian pushed her way aboard. Rolfe Trenier, the owner and operator of the boat – his livelihood – blanched at each unfamiliar new sound of the boat's distress and motioned with hands and arms as though he were a magician trying to make them all disappear. Not only were each and every one of his gray- and white-haired passengers overweight, they had been into the banana daiquiris and pina coladas since ten that morning and were now fairly frisky for their ages. The catamaran crept away from the dock, the surface of the water just inches from spilling aboard. The seniors rode it like a subway car, hanging on to parts of the boat and parts of each other, leaning out fearlessly over the water. At the top of their lungs, still healthy after all these years, they wailed out a recent calypso tune they had picked up from the islanders: "Judy drownded, Judy drownded; everybody call out, Judy drownded."

Sea monster fever, percolating a bit after Leland Armbrewster's press release, burst into full bubble when Rolfe, the catamaran and the ten old folks failed to return that evening. And by the following morning, at least eight islanders had vivid accounts of having seen the monster chomp the old folks boat in half and enjoy a grisly meal.

A sleepy lagoon, barely touched by civilization, where natives enjoy a simple existence without technology, traffic and turmoil, and half-clad beauties roam the beach. But now this little bit of paradise is also a scientific focal point. Maintaining its simple ways while providing for the thundering herds of biologists, paleontologists and monster lovers who hope to glimpse the Booby Bay Creature, Soleil reaches out to the world. It is truly an undiscovered Eden, yet with ample lodging and a casino under construction.

"Sidney Rouman. You know me of course." The larger and more pompous than life director swirled his cape.

"Why is this weird white dude wearing a cape?" whispered one bystander in a bathing suit to another bystander in a bathing suit. Do you suppose he's going to fly?"

"My flatterers call me El Sid."

"Uh, Mr. Sid," mumbled Leland. "So glad you could make it."

"And make it I have," said El Sid. "You are, of course, familiar with my epic of searing, but gentle eroticism, Summer of My Puberty. And here is the star of that opus, Rainbeaux Derriere – a little older now, a lot wiser."

"Pleased to be your acquaintance, Monsieur Leland," said the international sex symbol, dipping to display her internationally celebrated cleavage.

"She could speak no English when she came to me," said El Sid. "Of course, the film didn't have that many words in it anyway. I taught her the English she fractures so fetchingly now – and a great deal more. You might say I created her in a Pygmalion sort of way." The actress curtseyed. "You, sir, have requested a documentary on your local beast, an appropriate choice on your part, and I have come to deliver. If you'll introduce me to it, I'll get right into it. No sense dilly-dallying."

"I'm afraid it's rarely sighted," confessed Leland.

"Rarely sighted, eh," said El Sid. "That makes it more challenging. Well, I am no stranger to enigmatic and difficult stars. I relish the challenge. We'll just work around the shy creature until it chooses to show itself. I think I'll call the film *The Beast Who Loved Me*. The me being Rainbeaux here. Perhaps mostly Rainbeaux if the beast is as shy as you say."

"But it's a documentary."

"Of course."

It had been several months since the last creature tragedy, the devouring of the old folks, and Leland Armbrewster was worried. The tourists kept coming; he had maintained momentum with a steady stream of creature press releases. But they went home unsatisfied and Leland worried about bad word of mouth nipping this phenomenon in the bud. Loch Ness had established itself over the years, so even when people went there and saw nothing, the mystery grew. El Sid had taken over the old sugar factory for filming, but no one really knew what he was doing. He hadn't interviewed the locals, not even Chicken Avery, and he hadn't gone near the water.

Chicken Avery had gained the most in the past months and, to his credit, he was almost single-handedly keeping the creature legend alive. Tourists with little else to do were more than willing to give a buck to the only man who had faced the creature and lived to tell about it. And they got their money's worth because the story got better with each telling. Even Rainbeaux Derriere had paid him, not once, but five times, to hear his account, hanging on his every word and calling him Monsieur Poulet. She even accompanied him one night to the Crab Hole, where, after ten o'clock when Monsieur Poulet had transformed to Poulet au Rhum, they danced with abandon to "Cherry Pink and Apple Blossom White." Afterward they had strolled the beach naked and made love. In the midst of their passion, the beach moved beneath them and they were certain they saw the creature, thereby giving the Soleil tourist industry another few months lease on life.

Visitors were strictly forbidden entry to El Sid's studio, even Leland Armbrewster, the man who hired the director. But thanks to Chicken Avery, who had received a personal invitation from his friend, the international sex symbol, and who had allowed Leland to accompany him, Leland Armbrewster was now stepping into the magical world of Hollywood, or at least the Soleil version of it.

They stepped through the door and down into the two feet of water that covered the floor of the entire building. The floor underneath had been painted turquoise to give the whole place a tropical sea look. As astonishing as this was to Leland, it was not nearly as astonishing as what he saw when he looked up from his wet legs and across the large room. There protruding from the water was a huge gargoyle-like head with mouth open and teeth bared. And it was purple. Nearby, a purple arm also stretched from the water, holding out a flat hand, palm upward, on which sat Rainbeaux Derriere.

Before Leland could even catch his breath, El Sid, who sat in a director's chair also in the water, shouted "Action." The gargoyle's eyes jerked open and rolled back and forth; the giant arm vibrated. The bikini-clad starlet bounced in its mechanized hand, doing her best to stay aboard. Her bikini top suddenly exploded and fluttered to the water below. "Cut," yelled the director.

The arm stopped moving, and Rainbeaux climbed down and ran through the water to the two men. "Monsieur Leland, Poulet Cheri, isn't it exciting?" she gushed, as the two men just stared at her internationally acclaimed breasts.

With months passing without a single sighting, relieved islanders thought the creature had left their little paradise. But then late at night, its fearful countenance rose from the waters, eying two young lovers, who barely escaped its sinister clutches. With an entire ocean to plunder, what keeps this monster lurking beneath the waters of tranquil Booby Bay? According to scientists, the creature, in addition to devouring nubile maidens and assorted others, feeds on fauna unique to these waters. Accompanying this press release was a blurry photograph of a grotesque purple face.

The photograph had a strong legitimizing effect, and the Soleil tourist trade doubled almost overnight. During the day, pasty-faced visitors lined the beach; knobby knees pointed seaward, pina coladas held high. Every now and then an unknown something would disturb the serenity of the turquoise water, and a murmur would race up and down the line of spectators before the incident was explained by a passing boat or a dolphin or a swimmer. And the audience would return to watching and waiting.

At night, the braver of the tourists would venture out into local nightspots – even places such as the Crab Hole, where "Cherry Pink and Apple Blossom White" had been superseded by "The Adventures of Chicken Avery." Leland Armbrewster would dream dollar signs.

The night before Leland Armbrewster's Day of Great Reckoning, El Sid announced that he would be filming one crowning climactic scene for the monster documentary, on location, at the beach, with a cast of thousands, and, therefore, Leland needed to assemble a large and photogenic crowd. Leland didn't know what El Sid had in mind and didn't like not knowing what El Sid –

whom he considered somewhat of a loose cannon – had in mind. Nevertheless, he agreed.

Throngs of anticipatory tourists were on the beach by nine, supplemented by a large contingent of islanders. Leland paced the sand behind them, unable to rid himself of this inexplicable sense of foreboding. El Sid was nowhere to be seen.

An hour passed and another. As it grew closer to lunchtime, thoughts of food supplanted the craving for a glimpse of the creature, and Leland feverishly scurried back and forth to keep the cast of thousands from breaking ranks. Still no sight of El Sid.

Finally at high noon, a biology teacher from Memphis who had remained more vigilant than the others gasped. And the others, turning back, also gasped as a giant purple hand, then an arm, rose steadily out of the ocean. It was huge and awesome, and it quivered in a rubbery sort of way. "Look," someone shouted. "It's got hold of someone. A woman." "A damsel in distress," shouted someone else, who, on closer inspection turned out to be El Sid, now here, there and everywhere, poking his hand-held camera at the amazed onlookers. The damsel in distress was, of course,

Rainbeaux Derriere, and the look of fear on her face did not come from her script. She clutched the purple palm as the beast shuddered and swayed in the brisk ocean breeze.

The arm stopped rising and started rocking. And then it listed to the left, slowly at first, but picking up speed. The starlet was hurled through space, and the arm crashed to the water, where it bobbed as though it were a giant purple cork and floated toward shore.

Even before the creature's arm was beached, something else stole the crowd's attention. A young woman walked toward them, laboring under the weight of a large abdomen. The islander's eyes grew wide as they recognized her and wondered aloud if she were an apparition. She was not. Judy was undrowned, uneaten, and pregnant. As she described the wild night that she was plucked from the water by that ne'er-do-well Popo, taken in his boat to a love nest at Brigand Bay, there to remain until the thought of fatherhood sent her paramour fleeing, the islanders listened with sympathy. The tourists were not amused.

And they were even less amused when a local policeman came to announce that the old folks were back from weeks of imprisonment at the hands of Rolfe Trenier. Leland did not wait around to hear the details of their rescue. As the old folks competed in loud voices, each giving his or her personal account of the ordeal of captivity, Leland Armbrewster closed his suitcase and placed two brochures on it. His finger moved back and forth between St. Vincent and Trinidad, finally coming to rest on Trinidad.

"A lovely place," he remarked to himself, as he hurried off.

MATILDA

It couldn't have been easier.

The Pooh-Bah's engine roared to life without protest, and Humberto negotiated his way past the other yachts attempting to outsway each other as a show of sovereignty over the Playa Marique harbor. Behind him, the Bacchanal Beach Club sleeping off a night of hedonism with a reggae beat became tiny and meaningless.

Odus, useless as usual, lazed in a deck chair, dead to the world. But Humberto didn't need him at the moment, and he enjoyed the solitude. He stood at the wheel as though he were the very proud – and legitimate – owner of the Pooh-Bah, as she plied the now glistening water. He whistled a lilt he had learned as a child on the streets of a less cosmopolitan Caracas. When he delivered this fine yacht to Caracas he would be rewarded handsomely. This time he'd take a little vacation. Buenos Aires, maybe. Or Rio.

Humberto's reverie was shattered by the appearance of someone who wasn't Odus – a young woman whose tousled blonde hair and oversized T-shirt suggested that until a few minutes ago she had been sleeping. She half glared at him through half-open eyes.

"Who the hell are you?" demanded Humberto, his eyes very open.

"Who the hell are you?" the young woman retorted.

"I asked first."

"I don't care. It's my boat." She paused. "Well, it's Harold's."

"Who's Harold?"

"None of your business. Get off this boat."

"Is that the son?" She didn't answer. "Or the father. You are a mistress to one of them, aren't you?"

"You animal. Harold is my stepfather. It's his boat."

"Of course," said Humberto. "I didn't recognize you all messed up like that. You're the daughter."

"Matilda," she answered. "Now who are you?"

"It doesn't matter," Humberto growled. "I'm in charge here."

"Like hell you are." She rested clenched fists on her hips, yielding not a bit. "You're trespassing. Just what are you up to?"

"I am stealing your stepfather's boat. And why are you here? You should be on your way to the volcano with your mama and papa."

"I was with Ramon. He left and I fell – hey, this is none of your business. Who do you think you are? My nanny?"

"Your parents, they will be worried. Damnit. They'll come looking for you, find the boat gone. I ought to slit your throat."

"You bet your sweet ass they'll come looking for me. The police maybe even the navy are probably after us already. You're ass is grass."

Odus stumbled toward them, tucking his shirt into his pants. "Hey man, who's the chick?"

"Don't call me a chick," Matilda snapped. "My name is Matilda. But don't call me that either. Just don't call me."

"Hot little chick, isn't she?" said Odus, staring at her and grinning. "What's she doing here?"

"She's a stowaway," said Humberto.

"I am not. I belong here. But you don't, and you'll both be in jail before long."

"Nice legs," said Odus, inspecting her. "I'll bet she's got a cute ass, too."

"God, you're slime," Matilda said, making a face to suggest she was about to throw up.

"You little bitch," said Odus, raising his arm to strike her.

"Stop it," said Humberto.

"Yeh," said Matilda, who had flinched only momentarily. "If I have any bruises when they catch you, you'll probably never see the outside of a cell again, that is if they don't shoot you."

"What's she talking about?" asked Odus, turning to Humberto.

"Our plans may have been fouled up, thanks to little miss hot pants here," said Humberto. Matilda smiled at him. "Let me think," he said.

"Oooh, that should be exciting," said Matilda. "Can I watch?"

Humberto stared at the sea ahead of them for several moments, then mumbled. "We probably got an hour or two on them, but they can overtake us. And they'll know we're headed for Caracas."

"Maybe they'll think she took the boat out," Odus offered.

"I would never take the boat anywhere without my stepdaddy's permission," said Matilda, looking toward heaven.

Thinking aloud, Humberto half spoke, half mumbled. "They're expecting us to go to Caracas. What if we went to Maracaibo instead? They wouldn't expect that. We could lose the yacht there. God, I hate to lose the yacht. It's worth a bundle. Could we hide it somewhere for a while? No, we've got to lose it. But what about the girl?"

"That's easy," said Odus. He took two quick steps and scooped her up in his arms before she could react. "Let the sharks handle it." As he carried her across the deck, she now twisted and flailed and fought him, real fear in her eyes for the first time. He leaned into the railing and held her out over the water.

"Stop," shouted Humberto. "We can't do that."

"Listen to him," pleaded Matilda, looking alternately at Odus and the sea stretching out below. "He's older and wiser."

"Goddamn it," Odus muttered, lowering her to the deck, but fondling her as much as he could before she was on her feet and hurrying toward Humberto, her unlikely savior.

"That would be murder," said Humberto. "Stealing is one thing, but murder is something else. That's bad. They catch us, they shoot us. Besides, we are not killers." The fear in Matilda's eyes disappeared with his words, and her composure returned. Humberto was not watching her, did not see the change in her expression. He didn't realize that he had lost command.

"I got an idea," said Odus, rejoining them.

"Wow," said Matilda, circling him, looking him up and down. "This should be good."

"We find a hidden cove, maybe on one of the coastal islands," said Odus, beaming. "Then we ransom the chick." He looked to Humberto for the almost certain accolade. Humberto stared back at him for a moment, then turned his gaze to Matilda, allowing the idea to parade through his mind for inspection. Matilda, on the other hand, laughed out loud.

"What's so funny?" Odus demanded.

"Ransom," said Matilda through her laughter. "Didn't you ever read 'The Ransom of Red Chief'? Of course not. What am I thinking? You don't read. You're thinking my stepfather would pay to get me back. The most he'd give you is a bottle of champagne and a thank you note for taking me off his hands."

"Your step papa doesn't like you?" said Humberto.

"Positively hates me."

"And your mama?"

"Well, she probably doesn't hate me, but she's more comfortable when I'm not around."

"This is not the happy americano family from TV," said Humberto, eyes narrowing.

"The Cleavers we're not," said Matilda. "Maybe Lizzie Borden and her family."

"Hmmm," said Humberto. "Then it's very possible that the entire U.S. Navy is not pursuing us at the moment."

"Whoops," said Matilda; then she shrugged. "You're right. I'd guess at this moment they're probably peering into the volcano, saying it's my own fault I missed it, if I couldn't be in the right place at the right time. So now what?"

"Caracas," said Humberto.

"Quit staring at me," said Matilda. She was lying on the big chaise lounge, letting the sun bake her. Her words took Odus by surprise; her eyes had been shut, and he had assumed he was unobserved. "You animal," she added, folding her arms over her breasts.

"Well, people gonna look at you, you lay around half naked. But that's what you want. You want everybody to look. Hey look at my hot little bod. Maybe you even want more than lookin', huh? Maybe them titties touched."

"I was minding my business." She pulled her big T-shirt on. "I don't want you to look, touch, or anything else. Except go away. Pervert." Odus clenched his fists and moved toward her. "Humberto told you to leave me alone."

Odus stopped and retreated. "Bitch," he mumbled.

"Asshole."

"So what we gonna do with her?" asked Odus. "If we take her to Caracas and let her go, she'll go to the police."

"Hmmm," said Humberto.

"There's a dinghy – little blue thing, just like the bitch's baby blue eyes. Maybe we should set her adrift in it. That wouldn't be killing her. And somebody would probably find her after a while."

Matilda came in from the deck just in time to hear his suggestion. Seeing Humberto entertain the idea, she quickly said: "But I'd probably die. I'm not very rugged. And they'd catch you and. . ." She pulled a finger across her throat. "Take me to Caracas. I won't tell anybody. Or I'll tell them you blew up the boat and they'll stop looking for it."

"But they'll look for us, " said Humberto.

"I'll give them phony descriptions."

"Why would you do such a thing?" asked Humberto.

"Because I really don't care if Harold gets his damn boat back. You probably deserve it more than he does.

He's an arrogant s o b. Look at the name of the boat –
Pooh-Bah."

"What does it mean?" asked Odus.

"It's his way of telling the world how important he
is, a high and mighty fart, a really super prick." Odus
laughed in appreciation of her description; Humberto
clucked. "Please take me to Caracas." She looked from one
man to the other with wide eyes. "You can trust me. I
know I was mean to you. But I'll be nicer, a lot nicer."

Odus frowned again as though he weren't buying
any of it. Matilda grabbed his hand and placed it on her
bare knee. "I know you liked the way I looked before out
on deck and wanted to touch me." Odus was sweating
now. "We'll have a good time before we get to Caracas."
She stared at him until he flinched. Then she turned to
include Humberto in the conversation. "All of us. I can
really be nice."

"Well," said Humberto, delivering judgment. "We
got time to think on it – until tomorrow afternoon – and
we'll still have the little blue dinghy if we need it."

"And we'll use it if you're not really, really nice
tonight," said Odus.

Humberto and Odus had already powered through a bottle of Harold's rum in anticipation of the evening and were speculating once again on the lengths to which their prisoner might go to avoid being set afloat, even though, Humberto promised Odus, she'd be set afloat anyway, when she emerged from below, radiant, slightly flushed, blonde hair neatly combed. She wore a delicate gossamer dress.

"Sorry I took so long," she said, smiling and sitting on the edge of a chaise lounge.

Humberto had killed the engines earlier, and the yacht now gently rocked with the movement of the water. "That's all right," he said, staring at her. "You're very pretty."

"Goddamn," mumbled Odus, staring as well.

"Thank you," said Matilda. "May I have a drink?"

"Yes, yes," said Humberto, pouring rum into three tumblers. The two men had discussed at length exactly how much they should let her drink so she might reach a peak of wild abandon, yet not pass out, although Odus had made it clear that her passing out wouldn't make any difference to him.

"It's a beautiful night," said Matilda, sipping at her rum. "So starry."

"Great night for gettin' it on," said Odus, grinning and gulping at his rum. Matilda smiled at him, and Odus accepted her smile as encouragement. "Great night for really gettin' it on," he added.

Matilda just smiled again, then lowered her eyes to her drink. Humberto and Odus downed their drinks, and Humberto filled their glasses. They watched and fidgeted as their quarry sipped in slow motion.

"How about a little chugalug?" said Odus, lifting his glass. "To a starry gettin' it on night." They all emptied their glasses, and Humberto winked at Odus who burped in reply. Humberto quickly refilled the three glasses.

Matilda looked around. "I'll kind of miss the yacht. But Harold will just get another one, so it doesn't matter much. How many boats have you stolen?"

"Six, seven maybe," said Humberto.

"So are you really gonna go through with it?" said Odus.

"Of course," said Matilda. "I promised."

"Well, when we gonna do it?" shouted Odus.

"Soon," said Matilda. "After I have another drink. I need to get warmed up."

"You get yourself good and hot," said Odus. He was sweating again. "I gotta pee first, anyhow. Save my place." He stood and walked away, swaying as though they were adrift in a stormy sea.

"I really don't like him very much," said Matilda, looking at Humberto through big eyes. "It would be better with just the two of us."

Humberto grinned. "He'll probably pass out any way. Here, we'll help him along." He poured more rum into his missing partner's glass and winked at her.

"Just us two," said Matilda, putting her hand on his arm. She spotted Odus weaving toward them and said more loudly: "And after you steal them, can you always sell them – or fence them – do you fence boats?"

"I guess so," said Humberto, also in a stage voice. "Sweet Leilani will pay $100,000 for this baby."

"Wow," said Matilda. "Who's Sweet Leilani?"

"He runs a saloon in Caracas," Humberto answered.

"He?"

"Real name's Jack McIntyre," said Odus, still standing and swaying. "They call him Sweet Leilani 'cause it's Sweet Leilani's Saloon. Why don't you take your clothes off now, and be sweet t'us."

"I haven't finished my drink yet," said Matilda. "But boy I'm starting to get anxious."

"How about another toast?" said Humberto, winking at Odus, then turning to wink at Matilda as well.

"Okay," said Matilda, raising her glass. "To the new owners of the Pooh-bah."

Odus raised his glass, rum sloshing, and said: "To my dipstick what's about to check some oil." He chugged the rum and leered at Matilda. "Momma, you ain't gonna know what hit you." He stumbled toward her, reaching out, fell to his knees in front of her and let his head slump into her lap. He remained there, motionless, until Matilda pushed him and he collapsed to the floor.

"Thank goodness," said Matilda, gulping the rest of her rum.

Humberto roared with laughter. "Just the two of us now," he said, also stumbling as he plopped onto the chaise lounge next to her.

"You and me," she said with a wicked smile. She pulled a small bottle from under the chaise lounge pillow, untwisted the cap and shook a small capsule into the palm of her hand. She tossed the pill into her mouth as Humberto watched.

"What's that?" he asked suspiciously.

"It's a real turn on," said Matilda. "These little things make sex cosmic. Want one?"

"I don't do that stuff," said Humberto.

"Okay," said Matilda. "I hope you can keep up with me."

"Give me one," said Humberto. "No, give me two."

"Two?" said Matilda. "I don't know. I've done two, and it's really a knockout, but I don't think you should. Not your first time."

"Two," Humberto demanded. She shook two capsules into his palm. He tossed them into his mouth and washed them down with the remaining rum. Then he began pawing at her.

"No wait," she said, standing. "I don't want to ruin the dress. Let's take our clothes off first. She pushed her dress off one shoulder. "Are you ready for more?"

Humberto didn't respond. He sat, the fingers of both hands frozen to the top button of his shirt, and stared straight ahead.

Humberto floated through space, doing his best to control the gossamer ship, but he couldn't, and large objects that were not gossamer slammed into his head, one after another. He was dying. If only he could open his eyes, maybe he would survive. He concentrated on his eyes and, with great pain, willed them slowly open. He could see only a shadowy blur within the blinding brightness. As the blur sharpened, incrementally in time to the pounding of his head, he recognized Odus, retching over the side at the other end of the baby blue dinghy. Beyond, nothing but water.

After leaving Sweet Leilani 's Saloon, Matilda went to the train station, where she fed coins into the slot on a storage locker until the door swung open. Over five dollars. What bandits, she thought, as she pushed the bag filled with $100,000 U.S. dollars into the locker and shut the door. Then she returned to the harbor. She noticed that the Pooh-Bah was gone already gone as she mussed her hair, ripped her blouse a bit, and staggered toward a policeman. Collapsing against him, she looked up into surprised eyes and wailed: "Call my Daddy, please."

YELLOW BIRD

A feathered kamikaze ablaze in reds, oranges and yellows, Antoine's bird plunged from the top branches of the tamarind tree. But then, at the last possible moment, it reversed avian gears and landed with a certain grace at the edge of the table where Antoine worked at his papers. It might have been a perfect landing were it not for the papers, but fluttering parrot wings scattered them.

Antoine grabbed several out of midair and, reaching down to the ground for the others, shouted: "Damn you."

"Damn you," responded the bird.

"Feathered fiend," said Antoine, stacking the papers.

"Damn you," said the bird.

Antoine suddenly grinned at the bird. "*Voila!* Your lack of vocabulary betrays your basic stupidity and demonstrates very well why I am at the top of the food chain and you are very near the bottom. At any time, should I tire of you, you are soup."

"Damn you," said the parrot, its voice crackling with defiance.

"*Fou!*" said Antoine, and went back to his papers. The papers pleased him, and he whistled as he shuffled them. The bird swaggered back and forth along the edge of the table. Other birds, coached by their owners, might declare themselves "pretty birds." Not this one. He knew damn well he was pretty and remained smugly silent on the subject. His human companion was himself quite smug; the papers on the table proved that he was profiting from the café against odds. Located at the center of the island, five kilometers from the nearest beach, Bistro Francaise nevertheless attracted a steady stream of customers. They came to sit under the fifty-foot tamarind tree for lunch and on his small patio for dinner. At lunch, the parrot swooped out of the tamarind to a tree pregnant with bunches of light green bananas, past a pawpaw, and over the diners' heads. He strutted on their tables and spoke to the lucky ones, sending them away remarking on the wonder of that bird. At dinner, Antoine strutted past their tables just to be sure they were in awe of his culinary ability. And after dinner he would sip cognac with them before sending them away remarking on the wonder of that man.

Not only tourists made the pilgrimage to the middle of the island; many locals dropped in to dine or just pass the time with a bottle or two of fine French wine. In a short time, Bistro Francaise had become something of an institution. Antoine was certain that this was a result of his congeniality as well as his culinary ability. Others, however, maintained that they frequented the Bistro Francaise because of the admittedly good food and the ambience of starry skies, crisp night air and the natural cacophony that surrounded them, untouched by manufactured sound, and that they did so in spite of the owner's "congeniality."

"You're a frog," said Antoine's bird, annoyed at the lack of attention. "God save the queen."

"I wish I could identify the swine who twisted your tiny parrot mind with this English prattle," Antoine hissed. "God save the queen, indeed. It takes a very backward country to not only retain a monarchy but to dote and gush over it."

"Jolly good."

"Go. Go fly away before I pluck your feathers. You annoy me." Antoine pushed his papers into neat little stacks and slipped an elastic band around each stack. He stacked the stacks, stood and marched toward the kitchen. Taking its cue, the parrot lifted off and ascended to the heights of the tamarind tree.

The Cuban black bean soup, amply fortified with sherry, was velvet on the diners' lips. The grilled grouper with hearts of palm stopped conversations short. And the gateau led to an almost reverential silence. Antoine beamed. He paced the periphery of the patio, sipping at a glass of the same sherry that had so transformed the soup, and puffed at a hand-rolled eight-inch cigar, always keeping a watchful eye on the two young women who hurried back and forth bewitching the diners that crowded around every one of the cafe's sixteen tables with not only their efficiency but their bashful smiles and the native lilt of their voices.

Antoine paused at a table occupied by four young men who were just finishing up. "Good fish," said one.

"Good fish," harrumphed Antoine as though the compliment were an insult.

"Did you catch them yourself?" asked another.

"Catch them myself indeed," said Antoine, shaking his head and resuming his circumnavigation of the patio. As he neared the end of the short journey, he spotted an attractive young woman sitting alone, sipping at a glass of white wine and staring out into the night instead of the book that lay open on the table. She had dark hair and dark eyes and the pale skin of a new arrival. A soft white blouse embraced breasts that inspired staring.

"Good evening," said Antoine with a slight bow. "I am Antoine, the proprietor and chef. I hope my efforts met with your approval."

She turned toward him with a tentative smile and examined him with deep dark eyes that rendered him impotent, tethered by her gaze. "It was delicious, thank you."

He paused, waiting to speak, afraid he might babble. "You had the grouper, I believe?" Easy assumption – only one person didn't have grouper – an American, naturally.

"Yes, it was wonderful."

His self-confidence was fighting its way back into the game. "Simplicity is the key with fresh island seafood. A subtle blend of lemon, wine and herbs, and searing heat. You are on holiday?"

"A little business, then a lot of beach. And, of course, dining." She raised her glass to him, and he beamed before giving his little cough that was meant to indicate a modesty that didn't exist.

"I hope you will be able to dislodge yourself from business and beaches long enough to join us for lunch. It really is a beautiful spot during the day. So peaceful, so unhurried."

"It must be. It's certainly beautiful at night." She looked out into the darkness once again and Antoine let his eyes drop to where the slit in her dress plunged between her breasts to somewhere below the top of the table. When he looked up again, he discovered that he had been caught. She was now looking directly at him, and her expression suggested she was fully aware of his indiscretion.

"Ah, yes, the night. It is beautiful. And you bring additional beauty to it, if I may say so."

She laughed a little and said: "Thank you."

"It is my pleasure, mademoiselle, my pleasure. But I must disturb your reverie no longer. I will excuse myself and return to my duties." He pulled to attention and stood as though awaiting dismissal, then said: *"Au revoir,"* and turned away.

"A demain," she said, and as he turned his head back, winked.

"A demain," Antoine said to himself as he strutted back across the patio, threading his way through the remaining diners without seeing them. *"A demain."*

"Bon jour," said Antoine, "you have returned." He held his arms out in an expansive, embracing gesture that suggested he might step forward and throw his arms around her. Instead, he dropped them to his side. "I am very pleased that you have come back and I am flattered as well."

"You knew I'd be back," she accused, leaning back against a post that supported the roof of the patio – rather seductive, thought Antoine, noting how her stance favored her figure, and rather reckless, given the condition of the structure against which she leaned. The simple blouse and short skirt were island skimpy but not as dramatic as last night's outfit.

"I hoped," said Antoine. "I only hoped. Please sit down." He was relieved that even though she didn't follow his suggestion, she did move away from the post. "All of the lunch guests have finished and departed. I'm sure, however, that I can find something in the kitchen to accommodate your desires."

Her dark eyes flashed with the suggestion that they hid more desires than he or his kitchen could accommodate. "I purposely came late," she said, and Antoine's heart raced until she added: "I had a breakfast meeting, so I'm skipping lunch. I came late so I wouldn't be tempted." Antoine stifled a sigh. "At least not by food," she said, and her eyes were once again toying with him.

"Then let us try to tempt you with something else," said Antoine, and he too paused with playful ambiguity. "Some wine perhaps?"

"You've done it," she said, laughing. "You've broken my will. I'd love some wine."

Antoine departed, then returned a few minutes later carrying two glasses and an open bottle of wine. He found his guest wandering just beyond the patio. "You're absolutely right. This is like what I'd imagine the Garden of Eden to be."

"But there are no snakes," Antoine said, sitting down on the edge of the patio and pouring the wine.

"There are, however, other tempters," she said, returning to the patio and sitting down so that the two glasses of wine were between them. "That tree is magnificent. What is it?"

"Tamarind."

She studied the tree, squinting. "I'm not wearing my glasses. Do I see a parrot near the top of the tree?"

"I'm inclined to think it is some scoundrel from the Middle Ages changed to a bird by a sorcerer," said Antoine.

She laughed. "I feel foolish having to ask. After all, I am an ornithologist, albeit a nearsighted one. I study North American species primarily."

Nearsighted, thought Antoine. So those deep dark eyes are not perfect in every way. "You're more than welcome to study that bird," he said. As if summoned by Antoine's words, the parrot descended from its lofty perch, glided toward them and came to rest, with much ado and fluttering, on the ornithologist's bare knee. "Perhaps," Antoine added, "you would like to dissect it."

The ornithologist was startled for only a moment by the parrot's arrival. She grinned at it and said, "Pretty bird."

Somehow Antoine would have expected an ornithologist to say something more meaningful to a bird.

"*Beaux nichons,*" the bird answered.

"Hush," said Antoine, reddening. "He just babbles sometimes."

"I understand some French," she said, flashing those dark eyes at the bird. "You are a brazen bird."

"*Beaux nichons,*" said the parrot. "*Beaux nichons.*"

"I apologize for the bird's complete lack of civility and taste."

"It's all right," she said with a giggle. "After all, he's French."

"I assure you there is not a single French feather on that vile bird. He speaks French only to embarrass me. Probably taught to him by an Englishman. His pronunciation is appalling. Apologize to Mademoiselle . . . Goodness me, I'm afraid I have inadvertently failed to inquire for your name."

"Rachel," she said, smiling back at him while she stroked the bird's head.

"Rachel," said Antoine. "A lovely name, but one would expect that."

"Rachel," said the bird.

"See," said Rachel. "The old bird's not hopelessly bad."

"*Beaux nichons*," said the bird, and with another dramatic fluttering of wings, it lifted off toward the tamarind tree.

They sipped at their wine without speaking, emptying their glasses, and Antoine quickly refilled them. "The parrot's coloring is quite remarkable," said Rachel, and Antoine suspected that ornithology had erased any thoughts of romance. "I think it might be quite rare."

"I would hope so."

"I mean it might be endangered. I have a colleague that would know for sure. I'd like to bring him by. He knows tropical birds. He's been working in the islands for years – most recently in Martinique."

"Ah, he's French," said Antoine.

"No, he's not."

Antoine shrugged. "He can be forgiven for that."

"I'm afraid he's English."

"He can't be forgiven for that. Only pitied."

Rachel laughed. "You're such a chauvinist. He's a very intelligent man. He has some great ideas about how to repopulate endangered species."

"I once knew an Englishman who had an idea," Antoine mused. "His head exploded."

"Stop," she said and leaned into him, but before he could respond, she was on her feet.

"Bring him by," said Antoine. "If it means your returning, I'll gladly suffer anything."

She laughed and kissed him on the cheek, lingering just slightly, before quickly turning and departing.

"You were absolutely reprehensible," said Antoine, staring at the strutting bird. "Pretty bird, my ass."

The parrot cocked his head to one side, looked at Antoine as though seeking forgiveness but said: "God save the Queen."

"The lady is an ornithologist. Do you know what ornithologists do? They eat birds – especially parrots."

"Polly want a fucking cracker."

"A rather attractive ornithologist," Antoine continued. "I thought all scientists were dowdy. Like the English – all tweed and no substance. Tweed. One shudders at the thought. Yes, an attractive ornithologist. I think I would like to have a liaison with the ornithologist with the deep dark eyes and *beaux nichons*."

"*Beaux nichons.*"

"Ah bird, you are no stranger to such liaisons, are you? Yes, I remember that yellow bird and how shamelessly you behaved with her."

The English ornithologist did not wear tweed; he wore casual island attire and was tan, not pasty. Rachel, Antoine noted, was doing her level best to hide her beauty. Prim shirt and slacks hid beaux nichons; dowdy glasses framed dark eyes; and her hair was pulled up into one of those buns that so titillate the English. She was attired for her fellow ornithologist, not Antoine. They sat at a table near the edge of the patio looking out at the tamarind tree.

Antoine brought a bottle of wine to the table and placed it between them. "Compliments of the house."

"Please," said Rachel with a disarming smile that softened the severity of the glasses and bun, "sit with us."

"Thank you," said Antoine. "But only for a moment. The lunch patrons will be arriving shortly and I must prepare."

"Antoine," said Rachel, "this is Arnold Covington. Arnold, this is my friend Antoine." The two men nodded at each other, as Antoine sat and poured wine for his guests.

He filled Rachel's glass, then turned to Covington, but Covington stretched his hand over the top of the glass and said: "None for me, thank you. I don't drink."

Antoine clucked as he pulled Covington's glass back and filled it for himself. "You are from Martinique, I am told. A lovely place."

"Do you think so?" said Covington. "I'm afraid I find it wanting."

"There's the parrot," said Rachel. She pointed toward the top of the tamarind tree. "See? Up there."

Covington looked up at the tree and hummed. On those rare occasions when the English mind works, thought Antoine, it's noisy. Antoine stared at the staring Covington without attempting to hide his disgust, but then he felt Rachel's hand resting on his knee. He turned to her and her smile at once melted his anger, and it said to him: *"I know this man's a complete ass. He's a bore and I'm sorry I brought him. He's a colleague and nothing more. He's not half the man you are. But that's to be expected isn't it."* And Antoine felt better.

Covington continued to stare at the tree.

"Do you think he'll fly down here, Antoine?" asked Rachel. "He did yesterday."

Antoine shrugged. "Who's to say? The bird has a mind of its own." But he was now satisfied that the bird had no intention of cooperating with the English ornithologist. Undaunted, Covington pulled a small pair of binoculars from his pocket, put them to his eyes, and continued to study the bird.

"Psittacus antilles vulgaria," said Covington after a few minutes. "The pronounced yellowness of the head, the squareness of the tail – no question about it, it's an Antilles Parrot."

"Voila!" said Antoine, raising hands and eyes skyward. "I always thought it was a parrot." Rachel giggled, but Covington just glowered at him. "I told the silly bird he was a parrot. He thought he was an eagle; but he's merely a sittingwhatsis with delusions of grandeur."

"He's not merely anything," Covington said with a sniff. "That's a very rare bird. Very rare. They're virtually extinct. We have four females in captivity on Martinique. But no males. Of course, I must take him to Martinique." Rachel and Covington both stared at Antoine who looked out between them at the tamarind tree.

"I doubt that the bird would want to go to Martinique," said Antoine, emphasizing each word. "I think he likes it here. I think he finds Martinique wanting." Antoine's remarks were lost on Covington who once again stared at the parrot through his binoculars. Rachel shook her head, and Antoine shrugged in return. Then, spotting a young couple sitting down at a table behind them, he jumped up and excused himself.

During the next two hours, diners came, diners dined and diners departed, singing the praises of Antoine and Bistro Francaise. The proprietor himself bustled here and there, keeping himself far busier than normal, never admitting to himself that he was avoiding the odious Covington and his parrot lust. Finally, only one table remained occupied, and Antoine was delighted to see that it was occupied by only one person – Rachel. They didn't discuss Covington or the parrot again until later that afternoon when they had departed the cafe in favor of a pretty, black-sand beach – a secluded stretch of paradise where, Antoine pointed out, one could take the sun in the French manner if one chose to. Rachel took freely to the French manner, and now Antoine sat admiring the subtle movements of her body as she talked.

"He's not that bad," she said. "A little short on manners, perhaps, but so are some others." Her dark eyes flashed at Antoine who just grinned. "And he is very intelligent. He's right about the parrot. If they aren't bred, they'll disappear forever." She leaned back to let the sun and Antoine's steady gaze caress her.

"Do you have a relationship?" asked Antoine.

"Do you care?"

"I asked, did I not?"

"Professional."

"You have rebuffed him?"

"There hasn't been any need to. He's never attempted to move the relationship beyond professional."

"He is a fool."

Rachel leaned toward him and let the deep dark eyes do their thing. "Thank you," she said. "At least I think that was a compliment."

"A statement of fact. The man must be nearly dead to ignore such a companion to study a wretched bird in a tree."

"A Frenchman, however, would ignore the bird, lure her to a romantic beach, coax her out of her clothes . . ."

"But of course," said Antoine, clapping his hands.

"And?" said Rachel, letting her dark eyes drop downward in mock innocence.

"Beaches are for lovemaking," said Antoine.

"Are they now?" said Rachel, looking at him again. "You're a forward fellow, aren't you?"

"Life is short. So is your holiday. It leaves little time for a cat-and-mouse courtship."

"So we skip right to the seduction?"

"Seduction is such a harsh word. I find you amazingly attractive. I think that you perhaps do not find me distasteful. Given those circumstances, I believe a liaison is appropriate. Do you disagree?"

"What about your bird?" asked Rachel, pulling back.

"I do not find my bird that attractive."

Rachel laughed and said: "No, I mean what about your bird going to Martinique?"

"Am I to assume that our liaison depends on it?"

"Of course not," said Rachel, riveting her dark eyes on him.

"I must think about it," said Antoine. "It is a difficult decision."

"That's all I ask," said Rachel, leaning into him until their warm skin touched and their liaison on the black-sand beach enveloped them.

Antoine was working at his papers when the bird made its usual showy entrance, once more sending a flurry of papers into the air.

"Damn you," said Antoine.

"Damn you," said the bird.

Antoine looked up at the bird and smiled an apologetic smile. "I'm afraid I have betrayed you, *mon ami*."

The bird cocked its head and looked back at Antoine. "You're a frog."

"Hurl your insults, little feathered friend. I deserve them. I am a beast. Base sexual desire has led me to cruel infidelity. Like a drug addict that will do anything to satisfy his craving. Willing to pay any price for a moment's pleasure."

"*Beaux nichons*," said the parrot.

"I'm afraid so," said Antoine. "I'm afraid so." He stared at the parrot, then broke into a grin. "But why do I say such things. It is not so. I have done you a great favor." He clapped his hands, and the parrot lifted its wings and stepped backward as though about to retreat to the tamarind tree. "My selfless liaison with the ornithologist with the deep dark eyes and *beaux nichons* has created for you a grand opportunity. You, lucky bird, are going to Martinique – a beautiful place – for a liaison with, not one, but four yellow birds with deep dark eyes and *beaux nichons.* "What do you say to that, ungrateful bird?"

"God save the Queen."

SWEET SUGAR CANE

"All of y'rise," said Victor Clovis who most of the time drove a taxi, shuffling tourists from one island rendezvous to another, but who, on the rare occasions when court was in session, served as whatever court personnel might be needed. Except judge, of course. Those duties fell to the short gentlemen who stood rather pretentiously behind the unpretentious teacher's desk in one of the three rooms in Ste. Catherine School. Student desks had been pushed to one side of the room to make room for grown-up folding chairs, and court was now in session.

Everyone in the classroom/courtroom did indeed rise as instructed, everyone being Regina Napoleon, her husband Corso, his friend Max Rollo, and a good dozen townspeople who had nothing to do on this hot summer day. Court proceedings were rare on the island, and they were timed to fit into the judge's semi-annual visits.

Mrs. Napoleon was the plaintiff in this particular case, her husband and his friend Rollo the defendants. She stood before a chair to the judge's right, facing, at about six feet away on the judge's left, the two men.

"Okay, be seated," Victor intoned, after the judge had seated himself.

The judge was not long on ceremony. Victor felt a little slighted that he was not given the opportunity to instruct Mrs. Napoleon on the matter of the whole truth and nothing but the truth before the judge started right in with questions.

"So you are charging the two defendants with attempted murder, is that correct?"

"That's absolutely correct, your most honorific sir, " answered Mrs. Napoleon.

"Even though one of them is your husband?"

"He's the worst of the two, don't you know. He's an animal."

"And they attempted this murder by immersion in a barrel of rum?"

"If that means they tried to drown me, that they did. That they did."

"Please explain."

"I was whacking some conch with a board – that makes them tender, perfect for conch chowder. I make a nice conch chowder, lots of conch and good vegetables – well they came in with big grins on their ugly faces and the look of evil in their eyes."

Defendant Napoleon stood and grinned at the judge. "I was drunk, you see."

Defendant Rollo rose and added: "So was I, that's the truth."

"We'll hear your story by and by," snapped the judge. "Now please sit. Mrs. Napoleon, you were saying the two defendants had the look of evil in their eyes. Do you agree that they were drunk?"

"Oh my yes," answered Mrs. Napoleon. "They were lit up to their very gills. I never like to see the two of them together, especially not when they're in their cups. And still they were drinking. 'There'll be mischief,' I said to myself."

"They were drinking from this barrel of rum?"

"They weren't, and that was odd. They'd take a drink from a bottle then pour the rest of it into the barrel until it was filled to the brim."

"And how is it that there is a barrel of rum in your kitchen?" the judge asked.

"Napoleon makes rum," Mrs. Napoleon answered, and then, glowering at her husband, added: "Very bad rum."

"Please continue."

"They were drinking and making strange talk. 'Kind of scrawny,' says the one. 'Not so much as you'd think,' says the other. 'I'd say not over 120 pounds,' says the one. 'You'd be surprised,' says the other. 'Ready?' says the one. 'Ready,' says the other. Then they stand up and stagger toward me. 'How much do you weigh?' says the one. And when I refused to tell them, they were happy about it. Grinning like drunk crocodiles. And the one takes me by the head and the other by the feet and they lift me off the ground. 'Stop, let me down,' I shouted. Napoleon just says, 'Hush, it'll be all right.' 'Take her shoes off,' says the other. 'And her dress.' 'We'll make allowance for the dress,' says Napoleon. I start screaming, and they dump me into the barrel of rum, right up to my neck." She shook a fist at the defendants and shouted: "You assassins. I want you hung."

"Please, Mrs. Napoleon," soothed the judge. "I know this is very trying, but if you could continue."

"I'll try," sobbed Mrs. Napoleon. "I was right up to my neck in rum. And Rollo says 'I guess we're set.' And Napoleon, the fiend, says 'oh no, we've got to count her head.' 'Well, push it in then,' says Rollo. And Napoleon pushed my head down and rum came into my nose and I knew I'd breathed my last and he kept pushing until my head was completely under and I saw the good Lord beckoning me and I said a last prayer that both of my murderers would rot in Hell and suddenly they pulled me out and I ran screaming into the night all soaked in rum like I was the one who was drunk. I ran to the station and told the policeman what had happened. At first he didn't believe me, thought I was drunk, but finally he followed me back. And there we found Napoleon and Rollo going at each other like a couple of wild animals, shouting about how many bottles of rum there were and how much that much rum should weigh. The policeman hauled them away and that's the last I know." She sat down exhausted but triumphant, and in what should have been a somber moment, the spectators, who had been giggling throughout, broke into loud laughter.

"Quiet please," said the judge, 'or I'll empty the class. .er . . Courtroom." They obediently reverted to subdued snickering. "Well, gentlemen," said the judge turning to the defendants. "I guess it's time to hear your version of these strange events. Prisoner Rollo, I sense that you're somehow instrumental in this curious business. Why don't you go first?"

Rollo stood. "I was drunk, your honor."

"I was drunk, too," Napoleon chimed in.

"I know that," said the judge. "Please continue."

"I am the owner of a drinking establishment known as Leeward Lounge. On occasion I purchase rum from Mr. Napoleon, because I know he needs the money and I try to help in my own little way."

"He pours it into bottles with fancy labels," said Napoleon.

"On the day in question," continued Rollo, "he came into my place at about noon and called for two drinks

which I served up. He said: 'this one's for you, dear friend.'
To be polite, I sat down and drank with him, and in turn I
produced two more drinks. He did the same again, and I
did the same again and so on – you know how it goes, your
honor."

"No I don't, but please continue."

"Well, it got to be evening and we were fairly tipsy."

"We were wicked drunk, your honor," Napoleon
interjected.

"Napoleon starts getting very serious and starts
talking about how he needs money for new equipment and
he just doesn't know what he'll do. When I show
reluctance, he suddenly says, 'I'll sell you my wife.' Well, I
was quite surprised. The woman is fairly unattractive, as you
here in court can see, but I've been without a woman for
some time and I was drunk, as you know. So I asked him
how much he'd sell her for. He didn't seem to have
thought that part out. I suppose the whole idea had been a
spur of the moment thing."

"And I was drunk," said Napoleon.

"He thought for a while then said 'I'll sell her for
two thousand dollars.' I told him I thought that was too
much and we went back and forth a bit. We somehow

reached the point where we agreed the price should be based on her weight, but we were both guessing at it, and we were a good thirty pounds apart. Being drunk, that didn't discourage us. It just made the whole transaction more interesting, a gamble. We finally settled on the amount of fourteen dollars per pound. Being a devoted husband, Napoleon insisted that the price be higher than the finest cut of beef."

Napoleon grinned and turned red.

"Since we knew of no way to weigh the woman, we devised an ingenious plan – well, it seemed ingenious at the time – to learn her true weight. In my business, I know rum. I know it by volume, and I know it by weight. Napoleon's rum weighs exactly 28 ounces the bottle. So our plan was this: We would put the woman in Napoleon's barrel of rum, and she would push rum out of it. Then we fill it up again, figuring how many bottles it took. And that would tell us her weight." Rollo looked smugly at the spectators as if expecting them to applaud.

"And the rest of the operation was pretty much as Mrs. Napoleon described it?" asked the judge.

"Pretty much," answered Rollo. "When she ran away I was a bit upset, but Napoleon told me not to worry.

So we measured the rum, and it was just what I expected. But Napoleon wouldn't accept this. 'It's not right,' he shouted, 'it should be more.' He began yelling that I was cheating him, and I felt duty bound to hit him. And he hit me back. And I hit him back. Well, you know how it goes, your honor."

"No, I don't," said the judge, "but go on."

"Then the policeman showed up and dragged us away and threw us in jail. And we were just drunk. We deserve an apology. We deserve damages!"

"Damages!" echoed Napoleon.

"Prisoner Napoleon," said the judge, "Do you agree with this account?"

"Yes," answered Napoleon. "Except for the part where he said Mrs. Napoleon was unattractive. And I'm sorry for my part in this, but I was drunk"

The judge sat silently for a moment, then said: "Given that Mrs. Napoleon was not harmed and that there was no intention to harm her and given that the two defendants have had several days in jail to reflect on their misdeeds, I'm going to release them with a reprimand and an order that they never drink together again. Mrs.

Napoleon, I regret your ordeal and suggest you might think of separation as a possible solution to your situation."

"Oh no, sir," she answered looking at her husband, who began to sweat and shake under her gaze, "Napoleon's not getting off that easy. No indeed. We're going to spend many, many long years together."

MAN SMART

Captain Petrullo was a very proud man. He had just been placed in full command of the army unit stationed in Passion Point, the third largest town on the entire island – five hundred men, all under his very own command.

If a man were given to strutting to begin with, being in command of a 500-man army unit would certainly encourage him to strut in earnest, which Captain Petrullo did, up Ponce de Leon Boulevard across Saltwhistle Street and back down Citadel Road, two, sometimes three times a day. He would nod with a certain aloofness to those who watched him in awe as he did his turn around the town at a pace that just hinted at military precision.

Since Captain Petrullo was in the habit of being watched, not watching others, he was not prepared to react to spotting for the first time Mireille, the pretty young wife of Mayor Horatio Hornblower Cervantes. (Mayor Cervantes' unlikely name was the result of the union between his father who claimed to be descended from the Spanish writer whose name he bore and his mother who claimed to be related to the English admiral, not realizing, perhaps, that he was a fictional character.) The mayor had married the lovely Mireille before she was old enough to know better. In her youth, she had been seduced by the stature of the office, overlooking the stature of the man, which was less than impressive by almost any yardstick. In fact, the man was vulgar when not in the public eye, his eloquent words giving way to a vocabulary of grunts and wheezes and snorts. All in all, the marriage was not a source of profound satisfaction for Mireille.

When Captain Petrullo first saw Mireille, his military veneer went AWOL, and he trembled as if he were the lowliest recruit in his own 500-man army unit. His gait became awkward as he passed her; when he tried to nod, his head danced on a rubber neck; and when he tried to greet her, his voice squeaked. The poor man fled up Ponce de Leon Boulevard as though he were being pursued by a 500-man army unit, not commanding it.

But the captain was a resilient man, and by the very next day, he was back to strutting. During his second strut of the day, he once again saw the woman who had done him such damage the day before. But he steeled himself for their encounter, and as they passed each other, they exchanged smiles. As the days passed, further smiles were exchanged, then words of greeting. Words of greeting grew into conversations, and the conversations became more personal. The words they dared not let enter their conversations were in their eyes, in looks that probably should not have been exchanged between the captain of a 500-man army unit and the wife of the mayor.

The flirtations continued to grow like the frangipani nurtured by the tropical sun until their passions broke the bonds of silence and spilled into the open. Neither Mireille nor Captain Petrullo was surprised that the other shared the same feelings, but each had a different reaction to them. The captain being a forceful military commander wanted to take action, to leap into the fray, to engage those passions as though they were advancing enemy forces that must be physically subdued. Mireille, on the other hand, being the dutiful if not particularly happy wife of another man to whom, no matter how vile he was, she had pledged herself, was determined to hold passion in check, to never speak of it again, let alone take any action.

And so, as the months passed, their affair remained innocent, for even though Captain Petrullo frequently begged leave to sully it a bit, Mireille stood fast in prohibition. But passion contained is not passion extinguished, and theirs continued to smolder, just short of the flash point, the danger of combustion ever present. To some degree, their innocence was aided by the lack of real opportunity to act without fear of being caught, but fate was not about to let the two lovers go untested. Opportunity, knock.

"Meeting in Port Charles tonight," grunted Mayor Cervantes one morning. "It'll go late. I'll stay the night." Perhaps if he had just said his piece, had not punctuated it with a loud burp, Mireille would not have decided right then and there duty be damned – passion, I am your prisoner.

Having made this momentous decision and later that morning encountering Captain Petrullo during his strut up Ponce de Leon Boulevard, Mireille informed her lover-to-be. Captain Petrullo was at once as squiggly and squeaky as he had been the day he first saw her. With his head bobbing up and down so fast it might lift him off the ground, he agreed to an encounter that evening – after the Mayor had departed, after it had been dark and quiet for a while.

Captain Petrullo spent most of that afternoon grooming himself into the spit-polished image of the perfect commander, the perfect lover, the perfect seducer. How wonderful, he thought – a perfect man making love to the perfect woman and, as a bonus, making the vile Mayor Cervantes the perfect cuckold. Once he had primped and pruned himself to perfection, he strutted up Ponce de Leon Boulevard to Fat Freddy's Cafe where it had been agreed he would wait, drinking absinthe, until summoned by his amorata.

And Mireille still intended to summon him as the sun made its unhurried journey toward the western horizon, even though she had had the entire day to get cold feet. She somehow knew that this was a monumental, now-or-never moment; were she to not seize this opportunity, she'd never bring herself to take such a bold step, if she even had another chance. She intended to summon Captain Petrullo right up to the point at which she pulled a sheet of paper from the desk and wrote: Come to me now. Yours truly, Mireille – right up to the point the phone rang and she heard the chilling words: "Meeting's been canceled. I'm on my way home. I'll be hungry." These cruelest of words were finalized by a most loathsome burp and the drone of the sudden dial tone.

Captain Petrullo had taken the rather arrogant step of assigning one of his 500 men to a post near the Mayor's house, specifically to carry Mireille's letter of liaison to him at once. And by the time the young man arrived at Fat Freddy's, just as the stubborn sun dipped at last into the sea, Captain Petrullo, whose absinthe had certainly made his heart grow fonder, whose imagination had aroused him in every other conceivable way, sat in a state of intense anticipatory excitement. Thus it was with great agitation that he read words he had never expected, words that implored him not to come to Mireille's house, that her husband was at this moment on his way home.

A commander of a 500-man army unit must by virtue of his position, be bold and decisive, even when under the influence of absinthe and a now almost uncontrollable passion. Bold and decisive Captain Petrullo was. He stood and said in a very loud voice so that everyone in Fat Freddy's could hear: "This is very serious news indeed, Private Vincent. Go to the men and prepare them. I will assemble the unit at once. This is a night that will test our readiness, to be sure."

These dramatic words had their intended effect on the audience. Everyone sat in silence, staring at the captain, showing alarm. He surveyed them and remained silent for the longest time. Then the crafty captain said quite solemnly: "We have a serious situation which I am not at liberty to discuss. I deeply apologize but I must establish a curfew. Please go to your homes and remain there. No one can be allowed to leave – or enter the city tonight." He turned dramatically and marched out.

He marched straight to his 500-man unit and quickly placed them on duty at posts around the city with the most emphatic orders that no one was to leave or enter. No one, he repeated several times just to be certain they understood, instilling in them the notion that were someone to exit or enter the city, someone else would surely be shot. Then Captain Petrullo marched, no strutted, to Mayor Cervantes' house and to a very surprised, but very happy Mireille.

"But I am the mayor," insisted the mayor, to a little man with a big rifle who seemed to be hard of hearing. "If anything is happening I should be there." He tried to bully his way past the young man only to find the rifles of his two companions pointing at him. The mayor studied the two young men behind the rifles and concluded that they were determined not to let him pass and that they just might have the nerve to shoot their very own mayor.

Most of the other travelers who were turned away from entering the city found spots to curl up and sleep through the night. But not the mayor. He paced back and forth in front of the soldiers as though it were he on guard duty, and he cursed under his breath about the indignity of being barred from entering his very own city, for he did indeed think of it as his personal possession, and he did not like his sovereignty violated.

Of course his sovereignty was further violated within the city, at his very own house, not once but several times, after which Mireille fell into a Sleeping Beauty sleep until wakened with a kiss from her Prince Charming, or at least a strutting, military version of him.

The mayor paced throughout the night, until well after dawn when the soldiers were relieved of their duty, their commander having quelled the crisis that had threatened the city, the crisis that had required such drastic measures. The mayor hurried home, barely looked in upon Sleeping Beauty – not that he would have noticed anyway how much more peaceful, contented and radiant was her sleep – and went to the phone where he began making phone call after phone call to colonels and majors and generals.

By late morning, Mireille was flitting about the house singing, the Mayor continued to make phone calls in an effort to identify the scoundrel who had assaulted his dignity, and Captain Petrullo once again strutted up Ponce de Leon Boulevard across Saltwhistle Street and back down Citadel Road.

Unfortunately, Captain Petrullo's strutting days were numbered. The Mayor's phone calls did set some of the captain's superiors to wondering – and then investigating – the strange siege of Passion Point. And when it was discovered to be imaginary, poor Captain Petrullo was reassigned to lead a squad of six men protecting the gardens of the mayor's crazy aunt at the very end of Leeward Arm.

Mireille's detour from the path of marital fidelity had a salubrious effect on her ability to continue her life as the Mayor's wife. That one night of passion enabled her to once again become the faithful, dutiful wife without the need for further straying. Except for that dashing young sergeant the following year, and the lieutenant, Mireille remained – and yes, the twin corporals and the baby-faced recruit – but, for the most part, Mireille remained a quite proper Mayor's wife.

Don't Hurry Worry Me

As Chicken Avery liked to put it, "Clarence Henry's pants had a more exciting life than Clarence himself did." Chicken told the story of Clarence's wandering trousers with relish, and he told it frequently, because it was a good story and a story with a proper moral.

The story ended when Mango, Clarence's faithful dog, brought Clarence's pants to him a week after they had disappeared. The pants were soiled and wrinkled and just a little chewed up. Well, Clarence punished that poor mutt but he should have been thanking him because Mango was a hero not a villain. Of course, Clarence didn't know the details of that week during which his pants were gone. How Chicken Avery knew is anybody's guess, but he knew, and he loved to tell about it. And Chicken swore it was all true.

The story began when Clarence's wife washed his favorite pants, a pair of pale blue denims that had been brushed until they were as soft and smooth as the pink sands of Paradise Beach. She washed his pants, then hung them out on the clothesline to dry, out near the road where they were bound to tempt passers-by, being the fine pants they were.

And those pants did tempt a lot of folks who passed by, but those folks were honest, law-abiding citizens, and they resisted blue-denim temptation. All except that rogue Randall. He didn't resist. No, when he saw that no one was about, he snatched the pants right off the line, draped them over one arm and sauntered on down the road where he caught the bus that took him all the way to Port Elizabeth. From there, he walked up the road that led out of Port Elizabeth toward Titus Simeon's farm. Before he reached the farm, he ducked behind a bush where he slipped out of his tattered jeans and into his purloined blue denims.

"My oh my," he said aloud, as the softness of the blue denim caressed his legs and as he imagined how these pants would help impress Titus' beautiful young daughter, Ismelde, and how maybe she would want to touch the supple fabric and, thereby, the man within. He got quite excited thinking of Ismelde, her pouting lips and innocent eyes, and he quickened his pace.

When he reached the farm, he did not approach it straight on, knowing that he should avoid Ismelde's father who disliked the young men of the island in general and Randall in particular and who held the unreasonable notion that Ismelde should not carry on with young men, she being but seventeen and quite naive. Randall spotted Ismelde. She spotted him as well and pointed to the barn. Randall understood and quickly skulked into the barn where he waited with some impatience for Ismelde to join him.

Although it seemed as though hurricane season could have come and gone outside the barn while he waited inside, it was just a matter of minutes before Ismelde arrived, slightly flushed and very pretty. She was at once both disarming and demure in his favorite dress, the white one that hugged her the way he wished to.

"Look at those pants," she said, sitting next to him in the hay. "Aren't they pretty? And aren't you pretty in them." She rubbed his leg, and he shuddered with longing. And emboldened, he rubbed her leg in return, but only the part of her leg that stretched out from under the hem of the white dress.

"They're so soft," she cooed, caressing more and more of the blue pants.

"So are you," he said, letting his hand roam as well.

She smiled at him and whispered in his ear: "These pants are so nice it's almost a pity you have to take them off."

"Take them off?" Randall stammered.

"Of course, silly," she said, giggling. He jumped up and turned away as though he were a coward about to flee the enticing Ismelde. But, confused as he was, he really just wanted to get out of Clarence Henry's blue denims before the beauty in the hay changed her mind. He let the pants drop, picked them up, and tossed them cavalierly back into the hay. When he turned back to Ismelde he knew she was not going to change her mind because the white dress no longer hugged her. He stared at her, unable to move.

"Come down here with me," she urged, but before he could comply, a voice boomed from the front of the barn.

"Ismelde," shouted Titus. "Are you in there, girl?"

"Yes daddy," she answered, slipping back into the white dress as if she had practiced donning it in a hurry. Randall was not so calm. He didn't want to be here with or without pants when Ismelde's father arrived. He just took off at full speed out the back, leaving Clarence Henry's beautiful blue denims lying in the hay. Ismelde, realizing the pants were still there, crawled through the hay and buried them just as her father appeared.

"Girl, I just don't understand why you spend so much time in this barn," said her father.

She lowered her eyes as she pulled the straw from her hair. "Sometimes I just like to be alone, daddy."

At this point in Chicken's narrative, someone might ask, Chicken Avery how can you know about this? Randall told me, Chicken would answer and continue with the story.

Later that day, Ismelde carried the blue denims down to Port Elizabeth in a paper bag with the intention of donating them to a needy sailor. At first, she thought she might hide them until Randall returned, but then she realized it might be weeks before he summoned up the necessary courage. She thought of burying the pants, but couldn't bring herself to just dispose of the delightful denims. No, they'd be just right for some needy sailor.

"Does anyone here need some pants?" Ismelde asked the three sailors sitting on the dock, amusing themselves with beer and cigars. They eyed Ismelde with suspicion at first, then stared intently, their seafaring eyes inspecting her from stem to stern.

"I'd be needing some pants," said the largest and swarthiest of the three.

"Oh dear," said Ismelde, "I don't think they'll fit you, sir."

The youngest of the three spoke up. "I reckon they'd fit me." Ismelde studied him. He was of much the same build as Randall.

"Why don't you try them on?" suggested the other sailor with a big, toothless grin.

The young sailor stood and grinned back at his mates. "Let's do that. Couldn't take them if they didn't fit. Come on." He pulled a reluctant Ismelde aboard their sloop, leaving the other two sailors chuckling and speculating. A few moments later, a very red-faced Ismelde emerged from the sloop and hurried away. Just behind her the young sailor zipping his newly acquired, tight-fitting blue denims swaggered ashore, boasting to the others: "I guess she's never put pants on a sailor before."

Randall couldn't have told you this part of the story, someone would complain. Chicken Avery just shrugged them off. Now don't you hurry me, he'd say. Don't worry me. Someone told me this, someone else told me that. I just put it all together.

Three hours later, the young sailor was still swaggering, promenading the length of the deck, as the sloop plied the choppy waters off the windward side of the island. And perhaps it was that swaggering that rendered his sea legs useless against the lurching of the sloop, that threw him off balance and allowed him to be tossed off the starboard side, blue denims and all.

Elton Sinclair's hours of sobriety were few. And he spent those few hours combing the beach for clues to the buried treasure that would lift him out of the drudgery of island life and whisk him away to the upper strata of

European society, where he would drink cognac instead of rum. The corpse in the blue denim trousers lying in a heap on Pigeon Beach presented Elton with a bit of a moral dilemma. Should he report the body to the authorities and subject himself to all their suspicious interrogation or just let someone else discover the body and deal with the fuss. He realized that, if everyone who happened onto the body were to save themselves the fuss, the body would never be officially discovered even though everyone on the island must know about it.   On the other hand, he was a busy man; there were others with more time to waste on fuss.

Having faced the first moral dilemma and making a sound decision, Elton face a second moral dilemma. Would the authorities, once the body had been discovered by someone other than Elton, care whether the corpse was attired in a pair of handsome blue denims or in a pair of shabby brown pants much like those that Elton wore? Of course not. Elton knelt down next to the sailor and peeled the pants from his lifeless body. He was about to remove his own pants and put them on the body when it struck him that the poor wretch lying there was free of all care and certainly any care about whether or not he wore pants at all. So Elton saluted the naked corpse, slung the blue denims over one arm and headed down the beach, keeping watch for any telltale signs of treasure.

Every bit of island treasure still remained buried when Elton figured he had earned a break at the Crab Hole. He carefully draped Clarence Henry's blue denims over a large rock so they might dry while he wet himself inside. Those pants hadn't been on the rock ten minutes when who should walk by but that rogue Randall.

"My pants!" he said, remembering the blue denims but somehow forgetting their origin and rightful ownership. He scooped them up, went around back of the Crab Hole, slipped out of his pants and into Clarence Henry's snappy blue denims. They were damp, but still soft. Out of a sense of fairness, Randall stretched his own pants over the rock, before heading off to an afternoon liaison with none other than the wife of the man whose pants he wore.

At this point in the story, Chicken Avery was usually forced to quell a mutiny among listeners who said the story was just too preposterous. "Truth is stranger than lies," Chicken Avery would say. "Life is full of coincidences which maybe aren't coincidences at all but preordained or something." He looked up at the ceiling. "Now here's another coincidence. You interrupted my story just at the very time I finished my drink and needed a refill. So if someone would be so kind as to fill my glass, I'll get right back to this very amazing – and very true – story."

As foolish a person as Randall is, had he remembered whose pants he wore, he would not have worn them to this particular rendezvous. But he didn't, so he did. Fortunately, Clarence Henry's wife paid so little attention to Clarence Henry's pants that she didn't recognize Randall's blue denims as her husband's very own. And once Randall had arrived at Clarence Henry's house and adjourned to Clarence Henry's bedroom with Clarence Henry's wife, Clarence Henry's pants were a forgotten heap on the floor next to Clarence Henry's bed.

This particular liaison was interrupted in mid-passion by the sound of a door slamming. "What's that?" said Randall, jumping up.

"That would be Clarence," answered Clarence Henry's wife.

Randall, on his way to becoming something of an expert on hasty exits without pants, dove out the window. Clarence Henry's wife could have made her husband a very happy man had she just remembered who the true owner of the blue denims was. But she didn't, and she threw them out the window after Randall.

To Randall, the pants flying out the window were a Godsend, or so he thought until, trying to don them on the run, he was spotted by that good dog, Mango. Mango knew those pants, knew they did not belong to this young rogue. He chased Randall for half a mile, nipping him in the behind until Randall dropped the pants. Mango then gave him one last punitive nip and let the naked young man flee.

Then Mango returned those pants to Clarence Henry. But was he thanked for his efforts? Rewarded? No, he wasn't. That poor dog was punished.

But Chicken Avery had promised a proper moral. And a proper one he delivered, for Clarence Henry who had taken a stick to his one true companion would never enjoy those blue denim trousers again. By the time Chicken Avery's story had been recounted several times, Clarence could not strut around in those pants without everybody laughing at him. And if folks weren't laughing, it was because they hadn't heard the story. So they soon heard it, because Chicken Avery felt an obligation to tell them about the marvelous life those pants had had when Clarence Henry wasn't in them.

ANGELIQUE-O

Christmas is coming, the goose is getting fat,
Please put an explosive device in the old man's hat.
If you haven't got a big bomb, then a little one will do. If
you haven't got a little one, then . . .

Stop right there, Audrey, and try to practice what
you preach about Christmas spirit toward all, including
Grandpa Nathan.

Audrey looked around, hoping she hadn't been
singing out loud, making certain that, if she had been, no
one she knew was around to hear her. And no one was –

just the chattering strangers in the public market bartering their fruits and vegetables, a man whacking coconuts with a machete, and children playing football with a large jackfruit. Tomorrow was Christmas, an unusual Christmas, one that might well live forevermore in infamy, if they made it back to cold but conventional New England before reverting to their baser selves under an unfettering Caribbean sun.

The idea had originated during a nasty New England February, long after the memories of another family Christmas had slipped into an ethereal haze. As the temperature hovered at eleven degrees, Audrey phoned her sister Kathleen to float a trial balloon, her idea that maybe the family – she and Kathleen, Kathleen's "friend" Ron and her son Joey – ought to spend next Christmas somewhere south, put the money toward that instead of gifts that would, as likely as not, be inappropriate and unappreciated. "After all," Audrey argued, "the true spirit of Christmas doesn't require gifts or chestnuts roasting on an open fire. The true spirit of Christmas is being together as a family, so why not be together somewhere warm. Grandpa Nathan would be happy. He's always cold, and frankly I don't think he likes Christmas that much anyway. Let's just think about it."

Now, 310 days later, Christmas Eve, the temperature hovered at 83 degrees, and before hanging the damn stockings with care, Audrey scurried about the market in a quixotic attempt to find a turkey to cook for Christmas dinner because Grandpa Nathan had not missed a traditional Christmas dinner since 1943 when he spent Christmas on board a submarine in the South Pacific, saving the free world and everyone in it, including Audrey, Kathleen, Ron, and Joey, even though Joey hadn't been born.

Back in February, Audrey found a sympathetic audience. Numbed by cold and seduced by individual notions of tropical splendor, the rest of the family had agreed to Audrey's Idea, as it came to be called, thus giving her full ownership and responsibility. The others had just assumed that when Audrey said south she meant Florida, somewhere within waddling distance of Disney World, but Audrey was far more cosmopolitan than the others and was eyeing locales much farther south – Aruba or Barbados, perhaps.

After much study, Audrey settled on a little island in the Grenadines because it was "undiscovered" and appealed to her sense of romantic adventure. The others signed on because, being undiscovered, it was cheap. Only Joey balked at the choice, unable to understand why anyone would choose a dumb place like this over Disney World. But Joey wasn't putting up any money and therefore had no vote.

Maybe she could pass a really big chicken off as a small turkey.

Last Saturday, they had touched down to sun and warmth still holding the coats they'd had to wear to that other airport way up north. Entering paradise, Audrey was hopeful, Kathleen airsick, Ron wobbly on his feet, Joey comparing his fate to that of Robinson Crusoe, and Grandpa Nathan expressing his outrage at the price of airline liquor, fully convinced that the little bottles were meant to be free samples and that the flight attendants were pocketing thousands of dollars.

"Five dollars for a drink. It's obscene. We may be in a foreign country, but this airline is American and their employees ought to be subject to laws that protect us from this kind of usury."

"Yes sir," said the flight attendant forcing a smile. "And you have a nice day."

"Thieves."

"Why didn't you just let Ron by you a drink like he offered, Daddy," said Kathleen.

"Right," said Grandpa. "Shows how much sense he has, paying five dollars for something they're supposed to give away." By Audrey's calculation, Ron had spent at least thirty dollars on his own thirst. "And," continued Grandpa Nathan, "he's liable to end up my son-in-law some day, perish the thought, and bankrupt us all."

"The movie sucked," said Joey.

"Of course, it did," said Grandpa Nathan. "Cost a bundle, too. Just so you can be strapped into some infernal headphones like they're some kind of life support system. And for your generation they probably are. You're always strapped into those things. Probably being programmed. Subliminal messages: 'Kill all the old people. Kill all the old people.'"

Let the vacation begin.

When she finally found it, Audrey's spirits soared. It was a really big chicken. It might actually go pound for pound with some turkeys she'd met. And the nice gentleman with the missing tooth was willing to part with it for a mere forty dollars American, which seemed high but the man did have a large family in tow and after all it was Christmas Eve and she felt a lot like the Ebeneezer Scrooge at the end of the book – the rehabilitated Scrooge, the Scrooge who had happily forked over a preposterous amount for his Christmas goose.

But then the smallest of the man's children – the one who looked just like Tiny Tim – began to wail, because, as luck would have it, the chicken was the kid's best friend. There was no way Audrey could buy, let alone eat, Tiny Tim's friend.

And what could you say about the week? On the first day, the highlight of breakfast was Grandpa Nathan asking Ron through a mouthful of corn flakes: "My God, Ron, when do you not drink beer?" Not after two o'clock in the afternoon, after six of them, when Ron fell asleep on the beach and woke up fire engine red at five, in remarkable juxtaposition to the chalky white Kathleen who had lathered herself with sun block and cowered all day in the shade worrying about secondhand sun. Joey had been stunned into a deathlike stupor upon discovering that their accommodations lacked even the most prehistoric form of electronic entertainment. But on the other hand, Grandpa Nathan slept all day, and Audrey spent an idyllic day on the beach finishing a book of the scantest literary value.

At dinner, they were given menus devoid of beef and potatoes. Audrey found the fish chowder quite rewarding, but the others looked upon it as punishment.

Joey's catatonic silence was brief. Upon regaining speech, he did his best to emulate his grandfather and actually surpassed his skills as a malcontent. Joey was aided by the fact that Grandpa Nathan slept through the second day as well as the first. Ron cowered with Kathleen in the shade, and Audrey got a good start on another really bad book.

Having seen Grandpa Nathan only at breakfast and dinner for two days, the others were not as shocked as they might have been when, on the third, Joey came to the beach with an announcement. "Grandpa Nathan's dead." Audrey and Kathleen ran back to the house. Ron pretended to be asleep.

When they reached Grandpa Nathan's darkened room they tiptoed in, stood a few feet from the bed and watched. They did not have Joey's depth of experience with televised death and could not be so sure. But it looked like Joey was right. Kathleen stretched her arm and index finger toward the bed and poked the old man's cheek. She pulled her arm back and they watched. Grandpa Nathan 's eyelids fluttered and opened to reveal eyes staring at the ceiling. "Why in God's name are you poking at me, Kathleen?" he demanded.

"Well, we weren't sure . . ." Kathleen mumbled. "We thought . . . well, Joey said . . .that you were, uh, dead."

"Young Dr. Kildare said I was dead," said Grandpa Nathan. "And you, I suppose, were performing the autopsy."

No need for an autopsy on any chicken. The day they arrived, there had been a chicken in every doorway, a chicken in every pothole. Now the entire chicken population had fled, called to the sea like lemmings, perhaps, or led away by some misguided Pied Piper. The chicken she had rebuffed was the island's last chicken. But then, as she despaired, a man spoke to her from behind. "You want mountain chickens, lady? They're very good."

She swung around. "Mountain chicken? Valley chicken, beach chicken, chicken with lips. If you've got a chicken, I want it."

"Fifteen dollars American?"

"Twenty, if you've got one big enough for five people."

The man looked at her, confused.

"I need enough for five people." She held up five fingers.

"I got enough for six."

"Fair enough," said Audrey. "Nothing wrong with leftovers. Twenty American. There you go. God bless us, every one."

The man pointed at the cardboard box a few feet to the left, before pocketing the money and shuffling off.

Oh dear, is it going to be alive? She regarded the box as if it might get up and start walking around. She heard no clucking; that was a good sign. She hoped it wasn't alive. She approached the box and knelt down. She lifted the lid, just enough to peer in, and gasped when she saw the six creatures inside. Not only were the mountain chickens tiny and featherless, they looked just like frogs and, yes, they were alive.

Audrey wondered if maybe Grandpa Nathan hadn't had some kind of near-death experience that day they thought he was dead. Since that time, he had become a different person. He was almost cheerful at breakfast and dinner. He didn't complain about the food as much. And he particularly relished insulting Ron in ways that Ron didn't understand. He no longer slept most of the day, but would disappear with increasing frequency. Audrey discovered that some of the time he spent hanging out with the taxi drivers who were waiting for fares. They discussed politics, religion and island life. He knew them by name, knew how many brothers and sisters they had, and knew of their wives and girlfriends. They all called him big guy.

'Twas, as they say up north, the night before Christmas, and after the others were in bed with visions of sugarplums no doubt dancing in their heads, Audrey filled their stockings with the little gifts she had picked up here and there. And then she gave the Christmas gift that made her feel best of all. She hiked a short distance up the hillside behind their house and gave the mountain chickens their freedom.

The following morning, Audrey had the Christmas spirit, in spite of everyone – in spite of Grandpa Nathan who had been missing since early morning, in spite of Ron who was sleeping off his Christmas rum, in spite of Joey who had been complaining all day about the lack of gifts, and in spite of Kathleen who was in her room feeling sorry for herself. Audrey had the Christmas spirit because, just when the hope for a nice Christmas Day had been lost, when she had sunk to singing cruel Christmas carols about her relatives, a miracle happened – not a big Frank Capra miracle, but a miracle – a little boy who looked like Tiny Tim, bearing a big fish, a gift for the lady who had spared his best friend. And that gift inspired Audrey to cook up the best grilled grouper, fried plantain, breadfruit, callaloo soup Christmas dinner any New Englander had ever had, one that these particular New Englanders damn well better appreciate.

Audrey assigned Joey to rouse Ron and dragged Kathleen along with her to find Grandpa Nathan. They walked the beach shouting his name until they saw two figures approaching in the distance and recognized one of the pair as Grandpa Nathan. Then, as Grandpa and his companion grew nearer, Kathleen's mouth dropped open to release the gurgle of someone dying inside. Her eyes became swollen orbs as she stared at Grandpa Nathan's companion, a very young woman with bright eyes, a big grin and only half a bikini.

Kathleen swooned and only Audrey's intervention kept her on her feet as Grandpa Nathan chuckled, turned around, and pulled down his swimming trunks to reveal bright red buttocks. Kathleen regained her composure enough to pull Grandpa Nathan aside and demand: "Are you, you know, fooling around with . . ."

"Are you mad?" shouted Grandpa Nathan. "She's 19 and I'm 83. What kind of a sick old man do you think I am, Kathleen?"

Fortunately, Grandpa Nathan and his friend dressed for dinner, and it was served, with Audrey apologizing, even though she knew she shouldn't. "I'm sorry it's not turkey, but it's just impossible to find . . ."

The others scowled but Grandpa Nathan broke in: "Turkey? Why turkey? This grouper is the best fish I've ever tasted. And I love plantain. Turkey is for New England. We're in the Caribbean. Right Angelique-o?" His friend giggled and nodded in agreement. The others, reprimanded, stopped grumbling and picked up forks and knives. And Grandpa Nathan was right. It was a wonderful Christmas dinner, if Audrey didn't say so herself.

After dinner, Audrey happened to overhear Grandpa Nathan whispering to Angelique-o: "Of course I'll be back next year. I promise." And she thought, you'll be doing it on your own, fella. Then she thought a bit more.

Well, we'll see.

Everybody Loves
Saturday Night

Winter-weary tourists who take the considerable amount of trouble to get to Tortoise Bay are not thrillseekers on a hell-bent search for tropical carpe diem. They are bookish sorts, sun lovers, people who just want to slow down to the lazy tempo that prevails here. What little action there is at Tortoise Bay takes place on Saturday night at the only nightspot, Naughty Nora's. Nora's isn't all that naughty; the guiltiest pleasures are the flying fish sandwiches and rum punches. On Saturday night, the locals come to listen to the vintage jukebox play its unlikely mix of calypso, country and tunes that were popular when Bermuda shorts were still trendy. They come to socialize and to unwind after a week of work.

Some of the tourists also come to Naughty Nora's on Saturday night to wind themselves up just a bit after a week of lethargy. Given their low-key vacations, it's understandable that these folks might be a little overwhelmed at finding themselves smack in the middle of an invasion.

"Are you sure this is such a good idea, Claris?"

"This is the smart way to catch fish, Elton," said Claris with just a touch of superiority. "It's like that American dude that long time ago invented the assembly line where he could make a lot of cars at once instead of just one at a time. It's a fishing assembly line, and boy are we gonna get a bunch of them."

"But it's dangerous," moaned Elton. "It's dynamite. Someone could get themselves hurt. Like us."

"Not if we know what we're doing, said Claris, tying the sticks of dynamite into a neat little bundle. "We just float it on out there a ways, it goes bang, and boy it rains fish."

"Are you sure?" said Elton, skeptical of the raining fish part. "Have you ever done it before?"

"Not exactly," said Claris. "But I heard about it and got pretty good instructions."

He put the bundle of dynamite on the little raft and lit the fuse. Elton turned and ran down the beach as fast as he could. Claris, getting a little nervous now himself, pushed the raft out beyond the rocks with a long pole, then turned and ran after Elton.

Estelle Webster was working doggedly on her third rum punch, trying her best to feel comfortable in what she considered somewhat seedy surroundings. Her friend Penelope Goodwill had coaxed her into coming to Naughty Nora's, saying it was a good chance to see island life up close and for real. Estelle didn't need up close and for real; she rather liked the styrofoam ambience of a cruise ship, where fresh-scrubbed young men and women followed you around like puppy dogs, taking care of your every need. It was also Penelope who had convinced her to come on an island vacation, saying it would be more of an adventure than a stuffy old cruise ship.

Adventure. Here she sat while Penelope was standing around the jukebox with a bunch of locals, laughing and carrying on like they had known each other forever. Here she sat, enduring the unabashed ogling of a middle-aged hippy who looked very much like he aspired to nothing greater than beachcombing. He and his companion spoke French, although from her limited knowledge of French, it seemed as though they spoke it quite thickly – perhaps the result of the prodigious amounts of red wine they had consumed.

The third rum was better than the first. The drinks were a little warm; she had wanted ice but, upon asking, had been advised that the ice was not made from bottled water. She imagined a lot of people were careful not to drink the water in these places, but forgot about the ice. The filthy Frenchman was staring at her cleavage, once again Penelope's fault for talking her into wearing a dress cut low enough to get her arrested in a lot of small towns back home.

Penelope walked a little unsteadily back to the table and said: "How you doing?"

"Fine, just fine," said Estelle.

"You gotta relax, Stel," said Penelope, waving to the French hippy.

"Don't do that," said Estelle. "He's been staring at me, at my . . . just don't encourage him. He's French."

Penelope suddenly shouted to the other table: *"Comment allez vous, monsieur. Je suis Penelope. Elle est Estelle."* She pointed to Estelle.

"Allo," the man shouted back. "I am Francois. Pleased to know your acquaintance, Penelope. And you, Estelle." He put his fingertips to his lips. "How you say *bien montee, bien carrossee. Et un petit cul mignon. Tu es une allumeuse."*

"What did he say to me?" whispered Estelle.

"Good evening or something," said Penelope. "Just smile and say *merci.*"

"God, what if he comes over here," said Estelle, but upon saying the words she realized that maybe she wouldn't mind that so much. It was kind of . . . kind of exciting. Maybe this was beginning to become an adventure after all. She raised her glass of rum punch, but before it reached her lips, the windows rattled, the glasses and bottles behind the bar tinkled and Naughty Nora's itself – floors, tables, chairs, patrons – all trembled as if an earthquake were about to savage the earth beneath their feet. But earthquakes didn't usually come with a deafening bang, with the sound of something exploding in the night. Estelle's rum flew out of her hand and sailed through the air all the way to the French hippy's table, where it landed like a little aftershock. Estelle crawled under her table.

Naughty Nora's remained silent, except for the calypso tune on the juke box which persevered, unaware of the current situation, surreally inappropriate. Under the table, Estelle crouched on hands and knees, waiting for the next blast, the one that would end it for them here and now. She heard a little scuffling, and a fair-haired man appeared under her table, also on hands and knees. He grinned and said: "We can't go on meeting like this."

"What happened?" asked Estelle, her voice quivering.

"Damned if I know," said the man, who spoke with an English accent. "My name is Sidney Smith, by the way."

"Estelle," answered Estelle. Sidney Smith didn't answer; he was staring at her breasts. The lights went out. Estelle screamed.

From behind the bar, the efficient Nora quickly produced several candles and distributed them among the tables. The tourists at Naughty Nora's may have found a direct – and probably dire – link between the blast and the loss of electricity, but the locals knew that the electricity on the island was a fickle thing that would frequently take some time off. Saturday night was particularly prone to electrical problems since it was the one night of the week that everyone seemed to do things using electricity.

Everyone remained hushed in the flickering light of Naughty Nora's, speaking only in whispers. It was silent outside as well, but as they listened they heard a low rumble in the distance that grew closer but remained low and steady. A few of the braver patrons crowded around the windows and looked out into the moonlit night.

The heavy tank of German manufacture, which was the centerpiece of the island's defense forces, rumbled down Christopher Columbus Boulevard, followed closely by Her Majesty's Royal Militia. Although the island had long since severed its relationship with Britain, the militia remained her majesty's, and it proudly comprised the 37 islanders who owned guns. Accompanying them were another dozen paramilitary hangers-on wielding sticks. The great armored beast, its turret turning this way and that, had seen service in North Africa and was, therefore, the only member of the militia that had any combat experience. Nevertheless, to the tourists cowering inside Naughty Nora's, this was no Veteran's Day parade in Peoria. This militia confirmed their worst fears.

To the locals, now well under the influence of Nora's rum, the militia stirred their latent patriotic souls.

"We've been invaded," shouted Maurice, the bricklayer, breaking the silence that had held sway since the explosion. "The Americans are attacking."

"We should join our brave countrymen and help to repel the North American hordes," said Billy, the son of the mayor.

"We'll fight the Americans to the death," shouted Maurice, raising a fist in the air. Estelle, feeling very much like the wrong nationality in the wrong place at the wrong time, slipped behind Sidney Smith.

"What if it isn't the Americans?" said Everette, the taxi driver and voice of reason. "How do we know?"

"Whoever it is, we will fight them to the death," said Maurice, finishing off a glass of rum for emphasis.

"Yes," said Billy. "The Americans or whoever."

"But why would we want to fight to the death?" asked Everette, the voice of caution.

"For our honor," shouted Nora, from behind the bar.

"But isn't it better to be alive than to be honorable?" said Everette, the voice of cowardice.

"That's the attitude that keeps the islands under colonialist thumbs," said Billy. "What little we have is our honor, and you would strip us of that."

"But if the Americans kill every one of us, what good is our honor?" said Everette, the only voice of hope as far as Estelle was concerned. "Who will even know of our great honor? Will the Americans tell the world how honorable we were? I think not."

That was an argument that Maurice had to turn over in his clouded head, but in the meantime, he insisted, the tourists, particularly the Americans, were all prisoners of war. "We can't let them aid the invaders," he explained.

"Isn't it exciting," bubbled Penelope. "I've never been a prisoner of war."

Silent tension gripped Naughty Nora's as captors and captives assessed their situations. Nevertheless, island hospitality is island hospitality, and Nora continued to serve drinks to all. The rum and their unfortunate position as prisoners of war stirred up the embers of patriotism among the tourists. The British felt compelled to sing, and the battle hymn of the Boer War seemed apt enough for the Queen's drinking team:

"We are marching to Pretoria, Pretoria, Pretoria.

We are marching to Pretoria. Pretoria Hooray."

Upon hearing the vocalizing of the British, the three French tourists saw the honor of their country at stake. So with visions of Casablanca dancing in their bloodshot eyes, they joined the fray and their national anthem La Marseillaise thundered forth: *"Allons, enfants, de la patrie."*

Up to this point, the Americans had been somewhat loath to identify their nationality. But the patriotic crooning by their European counterparts had stirred the deep traditional need within the Americans to every so often declare their independence or at least best the Brits at something – not to mention the pesky French.

"From the halls of Montezuma," they roared, everyone except Estelle that is.

"To the shores of Tripoli. We will fight our nation's battles, the United States Marines."

A lone Australian joined in, wailing:

"Waltzing Matilda, waltzing Matilda.

You'll come a-waltzing Matilda with me."

The islanders were themselves no strangers to song, and they had soon joined the fray. Lacking the military discipline of the more war-prone nations, they took off in their own directions, each adding a favorite tune to the overall cacophony.

And so the vocal battle raged, the volleys of these plucky singing soldiers piercing the dim light of Nora's theater of operation. Like the greenest of recruits, these patriots made up for a lack of marksmanship by saturation – their musical bullets ricocheted from table to table, taking no prisoners, melodic shrapnel everywhere. Fight on, brave songsters, fight on.

"*Allons, enfants, de la patrie.* Pretoria, Pretoria.

This is my island in the sun. Pretoria, Pretoria.

Yellow bird, up high in banana tree. The United States Marines.

Waltzing Matilda, waltzing Matilda. From sea to shining sea."

Penelope stood atop a table, conducting the combatants. Estelle watched the less than perfectly pitched battle in amazement. She laughed, picked up a glass of rum that wasn't hers, downed it, and hummed along with whatever little morsel of melody she could extract from the din. A chunky little man stopped singing a Bob Marley hit and weaved his way toward her. He hulked his little body up as best he could until he towered beneath her. Grinning to display his handsome gold tooth, he gurgled. "Strip search."

"Not on your life," said Estelle, rearing back, but ready to use every little bit of self-defense technique she could muster.

Chauvinistic fervor soon gave way to the simple joy of music as the opposing armies found themselves conforming to one set of lyrics, singing off the same sheet, a lively if undisciplined rendition of the Banana Boat Song. Even Estelle, moving from time to time to avoid the man with the gold tooth, joined in on the raucous "day-os" that peppered the performance.

Necker Lincoln was certain his nose was broken. He was halfway to Naughty Nora's before the bleeding stopped. It just wasn't right. Sure, he had called Marie's momma a rhinoceros, but that was no reason for the woman to beat up on him. After slapping him some, Marie had tossed him from the porch of their house to the wet ground. And the mud and blood made him look as though he had – well, been in a fight.

"Daylight come and me wan . . ." Naughty Nora's hushed as Necker entered. Prisoners and captors alike looked at him in awe.

"Are you back from the front?" asked Nora.

"What?" Necker responded.

"The battle," said Billy. "Tell us of the battle."

"The battle?" said Necker, a little confused. Then he studied his own appearance. "Oh, the battle. I guess it didn't go too well."

"Oh my God," wailed Billy. "The bloody, bitter tragedy. The agony of defeat."

Maurice, who had not been singing, who had been sitting in a corner, dwelling on the infamy of such a big country as the United States picking on their little country – all the while lubricating his thoughts with a bottle of rum – stood and shouted: "kill all the prisoners!"

"Wait a minute, Maurice," said the still reasonable Everette.

"Yes, wait a minute, Maurice," echoed Estelle who, with all eyes now on her, regretted having spoken out of turn.

"Tell us more about the battle, Necker," Everette urged. "Were we badly outnumbered?"

"Outnumbered?"

"Yes," said Everette. "How many of the enemy were there?"

Necker grinned sheepishly. "There was just Ma – "

Estelle was the first to hear the same low rumble they had heard earlier. She hurried to the window, and the others followed, everyone crowding to see what was happening. Once again, the great tank crept down Christopher Columbus Boulevard, this time from the opposite direction. As Her Majesty's Royal Militia marched into sight, Estelle counted them, all 37 of them, followed by an even larger entourage than before. And they pulled a cart piled high with fish.

"Our glorious army has returned," shouted Billy. "We have won the war."

"We have defeated the Americans," chanted Maurice, jumping up and down. The two men ran out to follow the parade.

"The war is over," said Nora. "Peace is here. We hold no grudges. A round of drinks on the house."

Then, just as suddenly as they had disappeared, the lights returned, bathing Naughty Nora's with a kind of normalcy, with a peace on earth, good will to all. The jukebox kicked back to life. Estelle looked around. Tourists and locals had returned to laughing conversation. Penelope was flirting with the French hippy. Sidney Smith sat down at Estelle's table and resumed staring at her breasts. "What the hell," she said with a sigh, as she leaned back in her chair and sipped her rum.

The jukebox sang: "Everybody, everybody. Everybody loves Saturday Night."

7309972R0

Made in the USA
Charleston, SC
16 February 2011